La Gringa

Sidonia Rose Swarm

ISBN: 9781797432977

La Gringa

According to Merriam-Webster Dictionary:

gringa (n): *often disparaging;* a foreign girl or woman in Spain or Latin America especially when of English or American origin

La Gringa

"You know we keep that white girl, Christina Aguilera.
My jewelry too loud, baby girl, I can't hear ya."

- *White Girl*, Young Jeezy, U.S.D.A.

La Gringa

La Gringa

To my von TRAP family

La Gringa

1

The upbeat samba music lulled and the smell of scotch thickened. Ross grinned and winked at me across the table. "Once my divorce is finalized, I'm going to run through girls like you: beautiful and smart."

I rolled my eyes and turned my head to my boss, hoping he'd intervene, but I knew better. Jon wouldn't say a thing. Ross was our client and the owner of HealthVentures, a well-funded technology company. He could say whatever he wanted. I tried to redirect the conversation to something other than me or the fact I was the only female at a table lined with men decades older than me.

I could banter, debate, and hold my own in these testosterone-driven conversations, but this group was different. I was the only one who had any experience relevant to the monumental project ahead, making me a valuable asset. They might not have *wanted* me there, but they *needed* me there. Throughout the negotiations, I'd been doing all of the tedious, dirty work. If the project succeeded, these men would benefit directly, and my involvement would be an afterthought. I was a pawn in their multi-million dollar chess game with the Cubans.

Ross waved down the server, ordering a bottle of Macallan 25. He didn't ask for any of our input or preference. Just like he controlled the ordering, he controlled the conversation. If he wanted to discuss a specific topic, we discussed it. "Did you see what Melania did today?" he asked the table.

"Yes, I did," chirped Jon, sitting next to him. "I can't believe she said that."

"What do you expect when the First Lady is from Slovakia?" joked Ross.

I shook my head and corrected him. "You mean Slovenia."

"It's all the same over there," Ross stated. *If my only my Yugoslavia-born father had heard him.* I rolled my eyes and refrained from correcting him. I secretly hoped one day Ross might say the same thing to a bitter Serbian and get knocked out for it.

Jon must've seen the look on my face. He stuttered. "Soluna, your family is from that area of the world, right?"

"Yes. My dad's from Croatia," I responded.

La Gringa

"I was in Budapest last month," declared Ross. My head tilted in confusion, unsure of his point. *Did he think Budapest was in Croatia?*

Ross wanted to sound worldly and well-traveled; instead, he sounded like an idiot. Ironically, the time I'd spent in Budapest was the main reason why I was sitting at the table, but if I were to tell my story about my time in Hungary, no one at the table would care. I'd been to enough of these stuffy, client-worshipping meals to know that any contribution I made to the discussion would be interrupted by my boss, steering the conversation back to kissing our client's ass. Jon and my other mute colleagues — Chad and Pete — were more concerned with staring at my chest when they thought I wasn't looking than understanding why a twenty-five year old was leading the project they were assigned to.

I was unsure if it was the heavy pour of wine, or the fact we'd all been up early and working in Cuba that morning, but I began to doze and get less and less interested in the conversation. As my fatigue increased, my patience dwindled. Ross's stupid smirk and occasional winks from the head of the table started to annoy me even more.

"Budapest was not as cheap as I expected," announced Ross. "I ate at Nobu there, and it cost me three hundred Euros. Don't get me wrong…" He raised his arms for dramatic effect. "It was a great meal! But three hundred Euros! I thought that kind of money could buy you a wife in those parts of the world."

The entire table laughed in unison, because when a client cracked a joke, everyone was required to laugh.

"I think you have to go farther east for that," I added.

My boss nudged me under the table, signaling that I should stop contradicting Ross. Ross bringing up his experience of dining at a celebrity chef restaurant in Hungary was probably his attempt to relate to me, but his removal from reality just made him seem more of an asshole than I already thought he was.

I'd heard enough. I needed to extricate myself from this conversation. My memories of Budapest had more of an impact on me than some overpriced meal at a five-star hotel. I lifted the napkin from my lap, scooted back the heavy velvet chair, and proceeded to the ladies' room.

In no rush to return, I wanted my absence to last as long as possible without instigating any concern. As I threaded through the dining room, I scanned the groups of people dining at the opulent Miami Beach restaurant. One table looked like a United Nations subcommittee meeting that consisted entirely of supermodels. They seemed to have a representative of every ethnicity: a Polynesian man with a tattoo sleeve, a tall black woman with an incredible afro, a buff Asian man with an immaculate nineties boy-band hairstyle, and a Nordic woman in a trendy kimono-like dress. The unifying traits between them were their perfect bone structure, 0% body fat, and they were all 10s — Miami 10s. The 1-10 scale is unfairly skewed in Miami. A 10 in the Midwest is a 7 in Miami.

The restaurant's patrons served as an accurate representation of Miami — always something pretty to look at. I wished my group wasn't cloistered in the private dining room, so I might've had an opportunity to soak it all in. Moving through the candlelit dinners, I passed by a group of five jovial middle-aged Argentine men howling with laughter. I wished I'd passed by their table ten seconds sooner, because I'd missed the hilarious punch line of the joke. I had the urge to grab the bottle of Malbec from my party's table and relocate to this group, since they seemed to be truly enjoying each other — unlike me with my potato-shaped, corporate-drones.

At the end of my twisting walk, I noticed a young black couple sitting in silence who were both occupied by their phones. The woman wore faux diamond-studded heels that glimmered beneath their table. The man appeared to be on a sports gambling platform while the woman was holding her phone up to take a selfie and sticking out her tongue. I wondered if their meal was an hopeless first date or if they had been happily together for years. It was difficult to decipher.

How do these people make their money? How can they all justify an extravagant meal on a Wednesday? The local culture of projecting one's wealth, or illusion of wealth, shocked me. I was accustomed to supermarket-bought rotisserie chicken on a weekday evening, not five-course meals accompanied by three-hundred-dollar bottles of wine.

I arrived at the bathroom and felt a vibration in my purse. I reached for my phone. It was a text from my manager.

Hold your sass. We want the contract. It's not ours until it's signed.

I let out a sigh and proceeded to push the heavy bathroom stall open. The doors were made of solid marble accented by gold edging. The extravagant bathroom was a stark difference from being rationed the amount of toilet paper I could use in Havana's Jose Marti International Airport earlier that morning.

Growing up with my dad, he'd hoard jumbo packs of toilet paper. While I'd make fun of his stockpile, he'd attribute his strange behavior as a reaction to years under illogical communist mandates in Yugoslavia. His stories were inconceivable until I had the humbling experience of only being allotted one sheet of toilet paper. Even when I asked for an additional sheet, the attendant was only authorized to give me one. The rationing of toilet paper served as my abrupt introduction to real Cuban culture and the reminder of the realities of day-to-day life under communism. I never once made fun of my dad's toilet paper obsession after my first trip to Havana. An unexpected take away from my business to Cuba was the ability to sympathize and greater understand my dad's post-communist quirks.

Luckily, that evening's bathroom boasted a limitless supply of toilet paper in addition to dozens of toiletries and candies. I loitered in front of the sink and applied concealer. My worn face under my makeup served as visual proof of the long hours preparing analyses and catching early morning flights over the past grueling months.

I reentered the dining room and crossed the floor. The restaurant had started to empty out as the patrons from the other tables retired to the hotel's nightclub.

As I approached the men, I could already hear Ross's domineering voice. "Yeah, and that ass..." The men had apparently been discussing the physique of the stewardess from our flight. I couldn't leave them and expect to not come back to a sex-fueled conversation.

I wished I was invisible when they talked like this. Even though my cell phone's battery was dwindling, I assumed the stereotype of a cell phone-obsessed millennial. I held up my phone and began to mindlessly scroll, in hopes my table mates wouldn't pull me back into the conversation.

"Let's go back to my place," said Ross. "I've got to show you all my new bachelor pad. We can smoke some of the Cubans."

I turned to Jon, hoping that I could cut the night short. "I'm going back to the hotel."

"No," said Jon, shaking his head. "You aren't. Come on!" His stern face stressed that it was non-negotiable. "You're the young one, we should be keeping up with you. We don't have any meetings tomorrow, and I'll make sure you get a late check out. You're coming to Ross's."

I raised my eyebrow and narrowed my eyes. "Do these count as billable hours?"

Our departure from the table dragged on, because the men ordered one more shot for themselves. Once we finally emerged from the restaurant, Ross's gleaming white Rolls-Royce was waiting outside the hotel entrance. As big as the car was, there was no way we'd all fit in it. I offered to flag a taxi for Jon and me. Ross, it seemed, had other plans.

"Jon's a big boy. He can figure out how to get there himself. You come with me," Ross insisted.

Jon signaled with his hands and mouthed "Go! Go!" He'd been doing that for the past few months. While we chased the contract, Ross would suggest something and Jon would encourage me from the shadows.

I inhaled and reached for the car's door, but there was nothing in sight to grab. Ross clenched the handle which was located on the opposite side of most cars. I scooted into a back seat. Ross followed. HealthVenture's second-in-command, Juancho, hopped in the front. I shivered, trying to shake off the claustrophobic feeling. Being within a few feet of these guys kept me on edge.

We headed to a southern neighborhood of Miami, where Ross had recently moved into a penthouse of a mega-luxury condo complex. The twenty minute long car ride began with scotch-soaked small talk. Ross and Juancho's insecurities made them incapable of silence. During the meetings at their Coral Gables office and our routine trips to Cuba, these men always needed to be in constant conversation. They were too afraid to face silence and sit sone with their own thoughts.

Something buzzed on the right side of me. It was Ross's cell phone. I was relieved to know our chat would be put on hold. "Tell me some good news," he said, answering the call.

Juancho turned his head around to spark up a side conversation. "So have you been dating in Miami?"

"You're joking! Right?" I replied. "I haven't had the time. We just fly in and out for meetings."

"I'm not sure what you're looking for. Serious or not? But my single friends hang out at the Cigar Lounge on Coral Way. The guys there have money." *Is that all that matters?*

This was his way of trying to connect with me, by suggesting where I should go if I wanted to find a sugar daddy. While I wasn't currently on the prowl for a sponsor, I appreciated speaking with Juancho as opposed to Ross who was on the receiving end of a firing squad of a series of "yes and no" questions.

The car fell silent, apart from the man on the phone. The voice asked, "Have you done anything that would contradict your deposition...about not having any extramarital affairs?"

Ross turned to me to see if I'd heard the question. I pretended that I hadn't and kept staring at the colors of downtown Miami as we crossed the MacArthur Causeway. My gaze stayed transfixed on the hotel with a digital display of a woman's silhouette dancing. While New York City boasted the regal Lady Liberty, Miami's skyline had the looser version — a high energy go-go dancer — to greet its visitors.

Ross responded into his phone. "If I did, I took care of it. I paid a few broads' mortgages, car leases, and even put some money in their kids' college accounts. Don't worry, everything is fine."

"Jesus, Ross!" yelled the man on the other end. "Do you understand what's at stake? Fifty million dollars! Keep it in your fucking pants."

"I pay you the big bucks to be my lawyer," snarked Ross, "not my babysitter."

"Look," said the man on the phone. "Why don't you lock yourself in your fancy new condo, or go to an island. Better yet, go back to fucking Cuba, lie on a beach and just stay there until this is all over."

"Relax! Everything's fine. I handled it. They have no one to tell. Trust me," he continued. "They're taken care of."

I knew that Ross hadn't come from money, but he'd married into his wealth. His soon-to-be ex-wife Mindy was the only child of Miami's most successful real estate development family. Her family's company had been responsible for most of Miami's building boom during the late '80s. Now, Mindy was one of the area's best-known residential real estate agents. It was almost impossible to go a block in Miami and not see her blonde, smiling face on a billboard or bus stop bench. By the looks of her photos and pastel-centric wardrobe, she appeared to be kind and caring. I couldn't understand why she'd put up with Ross for so long.

"Do you have any more questions for me?" asked Ross.

"Good night, Ross," said the man on the phone.

"Good night, Jew boy."

The Phantom pulled up to the colossal waterfront complex, and a bellman escorted us to the suite's private elevator. Rumor had it, the only reason Ross purchased this specific penthouse was because it was the most expensive property on the market when Mindy had kicked him out of their home. Ross had contracted Mindy's rival realtor, Jill, to handle the transaction so Jill would receive the exorbitant commission instead of Mindy. Apparently the two women had a competitive rivalry to be "Miami's Highest Grossing Real Estate Agent". Ross's purchase had put Jill in the lead and ensured Jill would beat Mindy, Ross's real motive. The more I learned the details about his divorce, the more I learned how petty Ross could be. I wondered if he'd ever truly loved his wife, or if he'd always been a calculated money-driven sociopath.

Once the other groups arrived, we congregated on the terrace overlooking Biscayne Bay. Below us, million-dollar sailboats bobbed melodically underneath the moonlight.

While the men began to cut their cigars and pour more rum, Jon pulled me aside. I feared whatever was about to crawl out of his mouth. "Soluna, can you review the press release now?" He put his hand on my shoulder. I shrugged it away. "You always make things look pretty."

I gritted my teeth. I was the only one on the team moving this project forward and certainly doing much more than just making things look pretty.

"Yeah, sure." I celebrated the opportunity to excuse myself from the group. "I'll check it out now."

I retreated to the bathroom and locked the door. I pulled out my clunky laptop and slouched down to seek refuge. There I was, on the bathroom floor of a penthouse, finalizing a press release that would be picked up by the nation's largest news publications tomorrow. *Only in Miami!*

2

Shelley, Lauer & Co.'s Client HealthVentures Signs
Historic Contract with Cuban Government

February 12, 2017

Miami, FL - The United States could see a
shortage of more than a hundred thousand physicians
by 2030, impacting patient care across the nation.
According to the AAMC (Association of American
Medical Colleges) report, The Complexities of
Physician Supply and Demand: Projections from
2016-2030, there is a projected shortage of between
42,600 and 121,300 physicians.

Shelley, Lauer & Co. and their client
HealthVentures plan to address this issue by
increasing the capacity of physicians through
technology and seeking nontraditional sources for
employing additional doctors. While the issue of
physician to patient ratio is a growing American
problem, an island ninety miles from the United

States presents a solution. Cuba strategically trains more doctors than needed for their domestic use, and annually sends twenty-five thousand doctors abroad as a medical export. Between Cuban doctors practicing abroad, pharmaceuticals, and medical tourism, seventy percent of Cuba's export revenues are health-related.

With the counsel of Shelley, Lauer & Co., HealthVentures has established a partnership with CubaMédico, a subsidiary of the Cuban government, to contract Cuban physicians.

Shelley, Lauer & Co. Partner Jon Richards and his team have been advising and supporting Miami-based HealthVentures over the past several months during the contract negotiations. Richards explains, "Cubans in Miami will soon be able to consult virtually with doctors that speak their language, understand their culture, and ultimately, give them a sense of home when they need immediate medical advice."

Shelley, Lauer & Co.'s Healthcare Strategy Lead, Soluna Hill, is drawing on her experience of building mobile health programs in Eastern Europe to coordinate the elements needed for the project and optimize the patient experience. She explains, "With more American dollars flowing into Cuba, Cuban doctors have found themselves driving taxis, selling souvenirs, or taking hospitality jobs that cater to tourists." Currently, the highest-paid doctors in Cuba earn $67 USD a month — a government regulated salary. She continues, "With the HealthVentures and CubaMédico partnership, Cuban doctors will be able to significantly supplement their modest salary while, most importantly, be allowed to practice medicine and not be subjected to unskilled, tourist-centered jobs."

Commonly referred to as "The Miami Project", HealthVentures will use this contract and working arrangement as a pilot and model for working with other physician groups in foreign countries. HealthVentures CEO Ross Perkins elaborates, "While we are excited to begin the project in Miami, we are looking beyond and planning to expand services to the 1 million Mexicans in Chicago, 1.5 million Puerto Ricans and Dominicans in NYC, and the many other Latino people throughout the United States."

The telehealth services are projected to be available to the public in fall 2017 and will be offered through south Florida pharmacies who serve the Cuban exile community.

3

The text on the screen began to blend. *I need to sleep.* I closed my laptop and picked up my phone. Its screen was black. Upon leaving the bathroom, I encountered a surprise: everyone had left. *Thank God!* I went into the kitchen, hoping to find a phone charger so I could order a ride.

In the dimly lit kitchen, Ross was leaning over the kitchen island, devouring the remainder of a cheese tray like an opossum perched on a garbage can.

I hesitated, watching Ross. I felt myself becoming tense; I'd been left alone in the condo with him. I cleared my throat. "Ross, do you have a charger?"

He opened the drawer and shuffled around. He pulled one out, dangling it by its cord. "You can have it if you have a drink with me outside." His eyes were on me. "In an hour or so, we'll start to see the sun peek over the horizon."

I didn't acknowledge his proposal. I snatched the cord from his hand and proceeded to plug in my phone. "Where did everyone go?" I asked.

"There was some talk of going to the new club downtown. I figured it wasn't your kind of thing." The strip club was a natural progression for my teammates after a night of boozing, but I was confused about why Ross chose not to join.

"Why didn't you go?" I asked.

"I wanted to spend some one-on-one time with you. You know," he spoke, inching towards me. "Get to know you more."

Bullshit. His lawyer told him to lay low, and shockingly, he may have been taking his advice.

"I'm leaving as soon as my phone turns on," I said, avoiding eye contact.

"Would you share a drink and watch the sunrise with me if we weren't working together?"

I deflected the question. "I don't think we would have ever met each other."

"What's that supposed to mean?" he said, puffing his chest. "You don't think I am a good person?"

"That's not what I said," I quickly responded. "I just think we have vastly different social networks. I don't think we would've ever met otherwise."

Ross huffed and reached for the open bottle of scotch. He replenished his glass for the sixth or seventh time of the night. "So do you have a man in St. Louis?" He took a large gulp.

"No," I laughed nervously. "With my schedule, I don't have time for a boyfriend." I began to move away from him, leaning back to see if my phone had turned on.

"Good. Then no one will care if I do this..." he flung away his glass full of liquor. His rough hands grabbed my shoulder and scooped my back, hoisting me up. He dropped me down on the countertop; I jerked my head back and smacked it on the cupboard. My phone —— my lifeline for getting out of here — fell out of my hand, yanking itself free from the charger.

I shook from exhaustion, trying to push him away. "What are you doing?" I said with a tremble in my voice.

He let go with one hand, fumbling at his belt. "Giving you something that'll make you change your mind about having a boyfriend."

"Stop! I need to go," I demanded.

"No, you don't." he growled, his voice coming in heavy breaths. "You need to prove to me you're the right team for this job. I have a feeling when I'm done with you...you'll want to stick around." He pushed me towards the back of the counter, gripped my thighs, and leaned in closer. I shivered, my stomach turning, as he clumsily bit at my neck. He was treating me like his prey, not responding to anything I said. He was transfixed and ignoring my physical and verbal repulsion. With panic rising inside me, I twisted and fought against his hold.

I reached out my hands, flailing at the counter, desperately in search of something to grab. My left hand touched something made of glass, and I threw it to the ground. The delicate decanter shattered against the marble floor. Startled by the piercing noise, Ross let go and stepped back.

I took the opportunity and jumped from the counter. I was able to grab my uncharged phone and purse, but my shoes slipped off my feet. I left them behind and bolted for the door, pushing my way into the fire escape stairwell. There was no way I was going to wait for the elevator and run the risk of him touching me again. I ran down the forty floors to the ground level, throwing my body down the stairs in a twisting continuous motion, shoeless and shaking with rage.

Panting and exhausted, the stairwell spit me out into the building's fluorescent lobby. Ross was standing there, waiting for me with a glass of scotch in one hand and my ballerina flats in the other. He extended his hand while my shoes dangled. I snatched them from his hand and lunged towards the exit. Before I realized what I was doing, I spun around, throwing the flats at Ross like they were nunchucks. He ducked the first shoe and didn't flinch as the second shoe went wide. Both shoes ended up in the lobby's water fountain behind the front desk.

Ross turned to the security guard with a smug look on his face. "Hopefully she sobers up soon." *What a dick. I'm dead sober.* I drank one glass of wine three hours before.

I didn't need my shoes. The slight chance that my flats would graze and injure this pathetic excuse of a human being was worth more than any pair of shoes I owned. *But ugh! Those are my favorite! Why the hell did I do* that?

My fingernails dug into my palms. I pushed through the lobby's revolving door and bolted across the street to a taxi stopped at a red light. Just as the light turned green, I launched myself onto the hood of the cab, spreading my arms wide to block the driver's view. The car abruptly halted, and the driver rolled down his window. In a thick foreign accent he said, "Sorry lady, but I'm going home."

"No, I need a ride. If you take cards, I'll give you a hundred dollars for a ride to downtown."

"You serious?" he asked in astonishment.

"I've never been more serious," I declared.

The wide-eyed cab driver just nodded. "Yes, *mama*. Right away." Considering I'd pay with the firm's card and HealthVentures was covering all our expenses, I would've paid much more for this ride. As we sped off towards the city center, the driver turned and asked, "Lady, you want a charger?"

I reached for it and plugged in my phone. *Hurry up phone, charge faster!* Its screen began to glow. The moment it turned on, I texted Jon, Chad, and Pete.

WHAT THE HELL WAS THAT? WHY'D YOU LEAVE ME?

Right after I sent the message, a text from an unknown phone number appeared.

Let's pretend that it never happened. I don't want it to get in the way of the contract.

4

Miami's morning sunbeams pierced through the windows of the eastward-facing room. In my mission to get to the bed as soon as possible, I had forgotten to shut the blinds so the sun poured in, sucking the remaining life force from me. The light filled the room, and I rolled over to peer into the mirror. The jarring reflection was my mascara-smeared face. I hadn't dreamed the situation. The nightmare was in fact reality. I laid, hollow and depleted.

I mustered the strength to close the blinds and fell back into bed, welcoming the darkness. Memories of last night kept creeping back. The uncomfortable tossing and turning lasted for a half hour. I needed to occupy and distract both my mind and body so I headed to the gym down the street.

The cardio class began, and the bass of the blaring music prevented me from thinking too deeply. Midway into the class I felt the nervousness that was crippling my body begin to subside. I took advantage of the moment and closed my eyes, listening to the commands of the motivating instructor. While he was weaving though the class and telling us to "give it all we got", he tapped my lower back as a friendly sign of encouragement. His touch took me by surprise. My body flinched, and my mind jumped back, remembering Ross's grip on me, trying to keep me pinned. I couldn't control the tears that began to run and meet the droplets of sweat on the bike.

I dismounted and sprinted to the showers to let the tears flow. My plan of leaving the locker room before the class had finished didn't pan out. The tears overtook me, and my face found itself in an uncontrolled cry. Lockers began to slam, and neighboring showers turned on. My naked body trembled from anger. I turned up the water, allowing the hot water to pierce my lifeless, shivering body.

Twenty minutes passed. My fingers were pruned, and my tear ducts were drained. I stayed in the shower, not wanting to face anyone. Once I no longer heard nearby movement, but just the faint noise of blow dryers in the distance, I figured it was my chance to emerge without anyone seeing me. I slowly exited the shower and was checking my swollen face in the mirror when two figures popped out.

"Are you okay?" asked Keekee, her brows furrowed in concern. "I saw you start crying in class, and you scared me. You're always smiling. I don't like seeing you like that."

"Seriously!" asked Caitlin. "Is there anything we can do to help?"

"Oh my God," I said. "I'm so embarrassed you saw me. I didn't think anyone had noticed."

Keekee chuckled. "Girl, you made a scene! How could we not notice?" She gave me a reassuring smile. "But don't worry!"

Keekee, Caitlin, and I loved the early morning spin classes, and we'd started coordinating which classes to attend together. Keekee was a recent transplant to Miami. She was New York City born and raised, and new to town for a fresh start after a bad breakup. From bartending to the latest get-rich-quick scheme, she had a new hustle every week. Caitlin was from Ohio and worked as an investigative reporter for a local news station. The three of us were from very different walks of life, but we shared a common bond. We all enjoyed the same masochistic stress management: pre-dawn spin class.

It must have been written on my face; the way they looked at me, they clearly knew something was up. I didn't know how to explain what had happened. It was fresh in my mind, I still felt vulnerable, having not told anyone.

I decided to rehash the entire story — every single detail — in the gym's changing room, wrapped in a towel and with no makeup. I didn't care; I seethed with anger and frustration as I recounted what happened in the penthouse.

"That motherfucker," said Keekee, pursing her lips and shaking her head. Caitlin didn't say anything at first. Her job consisted of listening to people tell their stories so she waited until I was done.

"He can't get away with this," Caitlin stated, as she violently clenched her plastic water bottle. "I want to expose him so this never happens again. I am so sorry, Soluna. You don't deserve this."

"I know, I know," I said, as I began to fight a fresh onslaught of tears. "I'm just not sure of the best way to handle this. I don't know who I should tell."

For such a tiny human, Caitlin gave me a surprisingly powerful hug. Keekee's eyes swelled. She used her three inch long nails to swoop the hair out of my face and push it behind my ears.

"Wait! Ross?" asked Caitlin, letting go of me. "Ross Perkins? The husband of Mindy Perkins?"

"Yes," I replied.

"Damn, girl!" laughed Keekee and asked Caitlin, "Why do you know everyone?"

"Look, that's news," said Caitlin. She put her hands on my arms and held them tight. "This is your situation, but just know that if you ever wanted to bring this story to Channel Ten, it would be gladly welcomed. I don't typically mix business and friends, but know that it's always an option."

"Thank you," I said. "If it was any other client, I'd already have reported it. But…" I gulped. "This project means everything to me. I wish there was a way I could keep working on it, but have nothing to do with him ever again." The tears subsided, and I looked down. "Maybe I should put some clothes on now."

5

I gritted my teeth. I'd expected him to have this reaction, but hearing it out loud in the airport terminal served as a chilling reminder that neither he nor anyone I worked with cared about me as a person. They only cared about what I could do for them, their project and most importantly, their bottom line.

"Please, Soluna," Jon begged. "No one at the firm needs to know about this." He unzipped a small pocket in his briefcase and slipped his ring back on his hand. His finger was always bare when he was in Miami, but his wedding band found its way back on to his hand before he returned to his suburban home.

I stared at him, filling with disgust and disappointment. Disgusted, because he was flagrantly disrespecting his wife, the mother of his newborn child; and disappointment, that I ever thought he would take any action to support me.

"Telling anyone will just delay the contract," he explained. "Ross probably just drank too much because he was nervous about his divorce. He never put his hands on you before. Right?" He asked, but didn't want me to actually answer the question.

"Group One, Priority Boarding," the gate attendant announced over the intercom. Without wasting another word to Jon, I briskly stood up and walked away. I welcomed the upcoming three hours of solitude, and embraced the calming effect of being thirty-thousand feet above the world. At that height, problems seemed smaller, and individuals seemed insignificant.

While the plane was taxiing, I texted the only female partner at the firm. Despite only having worked together on a quick project last quarter, she always encouraged me to reach out if I needed anything. She insisted the women needed to stick together in the 'boys' club' of Shelley, Lauer & Co.

Hi Catherine. I need to talk to you tomorrow. Something happened in Miami. Will you be in the office tomorrow?

A text from the unknown number popped up. Barely twelve hours had passed since I left Ross's place. I'd already received twenty-seven text messages from him. None of which earned a response.

If you tell anyone about last night, I will make sure you never have a future in this industry.

The plane accelerated, climbing through the postcard-quality sunset. Dusk served as the time of day that we are humbled as the world asserts its supernatural strength, reminding us as humans that nothing on a canvas or screen will be as awe-inspiring as the sky opening up.

I pressed my face against the window and began to doze off as we gracefully ascended through the puffy cotton-candy-colored clouds.

The plane bounced onto the ground, and I jolted awake. I'd slept the full flight with my face suctioned to the drool-marked window. The outside of the window was now covered in frost. My phone had several messages.

Of course. Want to meet in my office at 5:30pm tomorrow? If there is anything you need from me in the meantime, please let me know.

Below Catherine's text, there were three more text messages from Ross.

It's a shame you didn't stay the night. It would make our work together a lot more pleasurable.

Respond to me! Dammit!

We will find another firm!

There was no logic in the bombardment of his messages. They were psychotic outbursts and threats which reminded me of the conversation Ross had with his lawyer. I realized that this was his normal way of taking care of "business" with the women he mistreated.

6

Throughout the entire next day back at the office, I stayed cloistered in my cubicle. My headset stayed on my head, while I pretended to be swamped in deliverables. I didn't engage or make eye contact with anyone. The moment the clock struck 5:30pm, I bolted to Catherine's office.

Her pink-colored room was an oasis in the middle of the stuffy office. A fluffy white rug lay on the floor, next to a driftwood coffee table. Tasteful art sat atop rose-gold shelves, and a life-size Buddha watched over the room. Every object in her office was placed with deliberate precision.

Catherine was on a phone call but motioned for me to sit on the couch. While speaking, she was uncorking a bottle of wine, pausing for a moment to scribble some notes. She smiled at me, holding up what looked like a peace sign and mouthing 'two minutes' before going back to her conversation. Doing several things at once seemed normal for Catherine; she laughed at something said on her call while pouring two glasses of wine. I didn't mind. The office was comfortable, and I spent a few minutes flipping through her record collection of Santana, Lauryn Hill, and other soulful 90's artists.

Her call concluded. She took off her earpiece and said, "I know you like Malbec, but I only had this Pinot Noir." She turned the bottle around and inspected the label. "If I have to pick the wine at a client meal, I always look for this kind. It's not too expensive, and most people like it."

"Speaking of being out with clients, that's what I need to discuss with you," I said nervously. I pulled my hair behind my ears and took a deep breath. Catherine put down her glass and gave me her undivided attention.

"Ross Perkins came on to me. Not just his typical flirty comments, but he actually forced himself onto me."

"Jesus," she said and shifted on the seat, settling in for a long conversation. "What happened?"

"He invited everyone who was at dinner to his condo. I didn't want to go, but Jon said I had to since I'm Ross's favorite," I said, rolling my eyes. "The guys were smoking cigars on his balcony, so I distanced myself to finalize the press release. Once I got back, I was the only one left at his place."

"Jon left you? He's pathetic!" she said. "Women would never do that to each other."

I explained the entire night in detail, from the faded bite marks on my neck to the thirty-four text messages I'd received. Catherine became increasingly agitated. She stood up and began to pace around her office, with one hand holding her wine and the other fidgeting with her Mont Blanc pen. She paused and turned to me. "Soluna, I'm so sorry you had to experience that. Please give me the weekend. We'll make a plan."

"Thank you." I nodded and repeated. "Thank you for listening."

"Of course. I'm going to tell Jon that I need you all next week for that Brazil deal I'm working on. Please just work from home. We don't need you here."

A smothering burden felt lifted; I'd been dreading having to face Jon and the others in the office.

Catherine and I spent the next hour chatting about The Miami Project and, if it was successful, what the potential was for working with other Latin American countries. I enjoyed chatting with Catherine, because there was a futuristic element to her thinking. Catherine was always one step ahead, strategizing and plotting the next move. We got so carried away talking that she forgot she was fifteen minutes late for her next meeting.

"Let's meet on Monday," said Catherine, following me to the door. "Say ten? At the tea shop around the corner? I'd like to have our next conversation off-site." She cupped my shoulder and offered a reassuring squeeze.

7

I bobbed my tea bag in the large mug while looking out into the blustering Midwest winter. I watched the morning commuters pass by. The strangers were too focused on their destinations to take the time to acknowledge the people around them. In the swarm of dark, grey-colored jackets, a smiling, radiant face emerged from the crowd and entered the cozy café.

"Morning, Soluna! Were you able to relax this weekend?" Catherine asked, removing her leather gloves.

"Yes. I finished the whole 'Narcos' series, and ate my body weight in Thai food," I laughed. "So yeah, it was a solid Valentine's Day weekend."

"That sounds like a great weekend to me. I'm glad you were able to chill," said Catherine. Unprompted, she gave me another hug. She must have seen the desperation in my eyes — the same overly expressive eyes that often got me into trouble.

"Over the weekend, I called each of the other partners; all of them encouraged me to sweep Ross' behavior under the rug."

"Go figure," I said, crossed my arms. While I'd hoped it wouldn't happen, I knew the partners would chose pursuing the contract over confronting Ross.

"We need to take matters into our own hands," Catherine paused. "I wish I'd taken a leap earlier in my career and built a business on my own. Instead, I've helped build many businesses for other people and have made them a whole lot of money. So I have an idea..." She excitedly stirred her tea. "You should leave the firm and execute the Miami Project as a separate company. Threaten to expose Ross, unless he signs over to you the rights to do business with CubaMédico."

I set down my mug down. I had so many questions. Catherine grinned. After a few stutters, I became capable of forming actual questions. "How would that be possible? What about the employee agreement I signed with the firm? Doesn't it have a non-compete clause?" I asked.

"I can rip it up," smirked Catherine. "As a Partner, I have the authority to terminate contracts on behalf of the firm. And I'd personally like to invest in your future company. The Miami Project will be successful, and I know you're the best person to make it happen."

I tilted my head and narrowed my focus. This wasn't what I was expecting. I figured that she was going to help me navigate the situation by switching me to another project or offering to write me a recommendation letter for a competing healthcare consulting firm. But I never thought of the opportunity to execute the Miami Project on my own and start my own company. The proposal was an unexpected curveball.

"I'll do whatever's in my power, to help ensure the success of you leading the project," said Catherine. "I talked to a college friend of mine, and she has a guest house for you to stay in Miami. I will pay the fee to break your lease, front all your moving-related costs, and invest fifty grand to start the business. I don't want anything to hold you back from this opportunity. Do you understand how big this could be?"

"Are you serious?" I asked in astonishment. "Of all the next steps forward, I wasn't expecting this."

"I believe in you," she said. "I believe in the project, but frankly, I don't believe in my teammates any more. I know the situation has been terrible for you, but please know this has been a very sad realization for me. My partners are douchebags."

I chuckled. Hearing a respected woman call a bunch of her business partners 'douchebags' seemed funny, but she was correct. It was the most articulate word to describe them.

"Don't repeat this to anyone, but..." Catherine looked around the café to see if anyone was listening. "I plan to leave the firm the day after my long-term compensation plan pays out."

"When is that?" I asked.

"In four hundred and seventeen days." She smirked. "Not that I'm counting." She showed me a countdown on her phone's home screen that read '417'.

"I'll have my lawyer make an agreement that forfeits the rights to do business with CubaMédico to you. You'll need to tell Ross that you plan to report him if he doesn't sign the document."

"Wait," I interrupted. My brain synapses began to connect. "I'm not sure if I told you, but I'm friends with an investigative reporter for Miami's local news. We go to the same workout class."

"Soluna, that's perfect!" laughed Catherine. "Why the heck didn't you mention that sooner?".

"I've had a lot going on," I smirked.

I gripped my tea to keep warm. Catherine took her hands, wrapped them around mine, and gave me a comforting squeeze.

"You know that you have an incredible opportunity if you want it. I'll tell Jon you're still working off-site with me for the foreseeable future. Please take the rest of the week off to decide if you want to move and if you do, start packing."

I gave her a big hug. "You don't have to do this."

"I don't *have* to," she reassured me. "I *want* to."

"See you soon, but not in the office. Go enjoy your day!" she said, pulling on her rabbit-fur hat.

Her departure was followed by the jingling of the bell attached to the door frame. I savored my final lukewarm sip of tea and bundled up. I pushed the heavy glass door, but it was held shut by the merciless February wind. I turned my body and forced my hip into the door, shoving it open. I took a step outside and the abrasive wind felt like shards of glass piercing my bare face. In that exact moment, I decided. *I'm moving to Miami.*

8

I pulled my hair behind my ears, securing my runaway curls. While most people complained of its effects on one's hair, Florida's humidity hugged my body in a comforting embrace. The dewy feeling and my puffy hair served as constant reminders of being in a foreign environment.

I fidgeted nervously as I waited in an oversized velvet chair in the lobby. Circular stone pillars as thick as redwoods supported the ornate, hand-painted ceiling. I surveyed the décor of the century-old hotel, preoccupying myself as I awaited the arrival of the rest of my team and client. The walls were trimmed with photos of presidents, celebrities, and dignitaries who had previously stayed at the Biltmore hotel.

A woman in a far corner played the harp, and her music was soon harmonized by tweeting noises from the center of the lobby. I stood up and followed the high-pitched tone to find a small community of vibrant canaries scurrying around in ten-foot tall cages. A middle-aged Haitian woman with a sweet face tapped my shoulder and said, "Excuse me, honey. It's breakfast time for my babies." She unlatched the cage's door and greeted the birds.

The chirping sped up as they knew they were about to be fed. "Good morning!" she called, beginning to feed the colorful creatures with delicately-sliced fruit. My attention was transfixed on a specific blue-grey canary burrowing its beak into its breakfast. The bird kept searching and not settling, apparently looking for a particular type of seed.

My phone lit up with a text from Catherine.

Good luck! I'm here if you need anything. Very proud of you!

I inhaled, hoping to gather all the tranquility and strength that one could gather in a single breath. I was minutes away from dropping a bomb at breakfast. The impending news would rattle Ross and Jon.

I heard a car pull up at the front of the hotel, followed by the slamming of a door. It was the Phantom that'd I'd ridden in just a few weeks ago. Knowing it was Ross, I hurried to the bathroom to ensure I wasn't in the lobby alone with him. I waited in the bathroom until I was certain Jon and the others had arrived.

Ross's eyes were glazed over, as if he'd just returned from a three-night bender in Las Vegas. I refused to look at him directly because his beady eyes reminded me that evil does, in fact, exist. Most importantly, I didn't want to get distracted from my plan — a plan that I'd been rehearsing over and over in my head.

I greeted the men in the lobby, and we walked in tandem to the courtyard where our table was awaiting our arrival. While we shared small talk about the weather, March Madness, and other frivolous matters, I made an effort to over-project my confidence. I wanted to dismiss any potential awkwardness of my first encounter with Ross since the incident. I showed no physical signs of discomfort; nothing that would remind everybody that the man across the table was capable of such disgusting behavior.

Immediately after the waitress took our order, I pushed my phone to the center of the table and said, "I want to show you guys something." Everyone was expecting a rather dull breakfast of reviewing the contract's formalities, so the interruption was welcomed.

The men passed the phone, sharing the photo of Caitlin and me.

"That's the blonde on Channel Ten," commented Chad. "She's an absolute smoke."

"Before spending time in Florida, I thought only hot girls did the weather," said Pete. "I didn't know they were allowed to report actual news." The men all laughed and nodded in agreement.

"Who's she?" questioned Jon.

"She's an investigative reporter," mumbled Ross. He unfolded his napkin and focused his attention on me, interested to see where my story was heading.

"Yes," I said, keeping my voice calm. "And she's also a good friend of mine." I directed my stare at Ross. "She's taken a personal interest in what happened three weeks ago between you and me."

Ross began to choke on his freshly-poured coffee.

"She wants to know why you stated in your deposition that you've always been faithful to Mindy," I said and redirected my stare at Jon. "She also mentioned she'd love to learn more about why the firm chose to pursue a lucrative contract instead of investigating a sexual assault."

"What's going on?" said Jon, squirming in his seat.

"Caitlin is planning to run a story this evening on the whale abuse at the Seaquarium, but I know she'd be more inclined to break actual news." I paused. "Like a recent development in Florida's largest divorce case."

I locked eyes with Ross. This was the first time we shared eye contact since the penthouse. I was in control, and it felt good. *Was this feeling of a disproportionate power dynamic, the same feeling that aggressors feel when they harass people?* I'd be lying if I said I didn't enjoy the feeling, but I wasn't harassing him. Rather, I was taking justice into my own hands.

"Today is my last day with Shelley, Lauer & Co. I put in my notice two weeks ago."

No one said a word. The men turned to each other, waiting for their higher-ups to say something. Soon all eyes looked to Jon, expecting him to intervene, but my focus remained on Ross. "I won't send Caitlin the screenshots of your threatening messages — on one condition..."

Throughout the past week, I had rehearsed this statement in the shower, on the plane, and minutes ago in a final dress rehearsal in the hotel's bathroom. Now it would no longer be in my head, but out in the open, making me vulnerable for its consequences.

I paused and reached into my purse and pulled out a small stack of papers. "I believe in the Miami Project, and I want to make sure it helps the people it set out to help. I won't say anything about that Thursday night if HealthVentures signs over to me the rights to continue the contract with CubaMédico."

Ross's Adam's apple slowly bobbed.

"You're making a huge mistake," Jon muttered.

"No, Jon. I'm not. Ross made a mistake when he put his hands on me and you made a mistake trying to silence me," I turned to look directly at Ross. "A mistake would be leaving the project under your control. I know you aren't in this for the good of the people, but for the cash. You have enough resources to make money in other ways."

I stood up, folded my napkin, and placed it on the table. No one said a word. All I could hear was the water rushing in the fountain behind me, and the chirping of the caged birds in the distance.

"Ross, it's your choice. You can sign the document and move on to a new venture, or you can be on the news tonight and jeopardize your divorce payout."

"Soluna," asserted Jon, "this is ridiculous. You think CubaMédico would work with a twenty-something-year-old?"

"I don't think so," I said. "I know so. I made sure of it." I'd called Yandel and Guido to explain that I'd be leading the project and Ross was out. Last week, the Cubans expressed their relief and excitement that *El Gordo* would no longer be part of the collaboration. "The project will continue, and it doesn't need HealthVenture's money. We both know money was the only thing you ever brought to the table."

Ross shook his head and nervously mimicked my behavior by folding his napkin. No one said a word, and a few long seconds passed. With nothing left to communicate, I figured it was time for me to leave.

"Since I'm currently unemployed," I announced, pushing in the heavy chair. "I'm heading to the pool."

They'd always had me on their team, but in an instant, I had just become their opponent. The typical social armor Ross used — his money and professional titles — couldn't help him in this situation. It was painfully obvious he was intimidated that I could intellectually run laps on him despite his three-decade head start.

Truthfully, I'd never have allowed Caitlin to break the story. As much as a sexual harassment case taints the perpetrator's reputation, the story forever follows the victim. Monica Lewinsky will always be Monica Lewinsky, the woman who blew Bill Clinton.

I didn't want any of this to be tied to my personal or professional reputation. The story could stay in my back pocket; as long as they believed I might still go public with it, it'd still give me the leverage I needed.

I escaped the air-conditioned hotel and entered the pool patio, allowing the warmth of the powerful midday sun to meet my skin. The aquamarine-colored pool was lined with bursting bougainvillea. The tropical trees surrounding the pool swayed in the light breeze, asserting their freedom. I zipped off my business dress to reveal a bikini — a premeditated decision. I waved down the pool attendant and asked, "A margarita on the rocks, please."

"Good morning, ma'am," he said with a smile. "Unfortunately, the bar doesn't open until eleven."

"No worries," I shrugged. " I'll take one at eleven."

I began to slather up with sunscreen. In the past few months, the only UV rays I'd been exposed to were the brief moments on the tarmac in Cuba. With my glowing fair skin having just come off a sun-deprived Missouri winter, I remained cautious in the intense, penetrating sun.

"Missy, I like your style," a peppy voice behind me said. "I heard you order a margarita!"

I turned to see an older woman with snow-white hair which perfectly contrasted her dark-spotted, leathery complexion.

"I deserve one. I just quit my job," I said.

"Good for you, honey! Life is too short not to be happy with your career. Kids your age are able to pick up jobs, leave, move, really do whatever the hell they want. I admire your generation."

The woman, who beamed a contagious, calming energy, pulled hot pink swimming goggles over her eyes. "I'm going to get a few laps in before any of those crazy little rugrats come with their floaties. It looks like we're cabana neighbors for the day. Maybe I'll get a margarita too," she laughed. "After all, I'll need some electrolytes after my workout." She daintily dove into the pool, creating a small splash.

I hoped that when I was her age I'd have that radiance. I put in my headphones and closed my eyes. I hadn't had a full night sleep in days, and quickly began to relax. Since my performance of breaking the news to Ross, my adrenaline began to dip, allowing my body to rest.

Nearby movement caught my attention, dragging me back awake. Hovering over me, the pool attendant held my drink. Next to me, the old woman had dried off. "Look up!" she said, pointing to a palm tree over the pool where five multi-colored birds congregated.

"That's them," said the woman. "Those are the parrots that escaped the zoo during Hurricane Andrew."

"They're beautiful," I said marveling at the creatures in front of us.

"I often think about their story. They probably had no idea the storm was going to end, but when it did, they were free and no longer captive. Must have been an incredible feeling…to be cooped up your whole life in a cage, endure a traumatic storm, and then boom, you're set free. They've been flying around as a flock ever since the hurricane." The woman extended her hand. "By the way, I'm Alexandra."

My new friend and I discovered we'd be neighbors. She was an artist in Coconut Grove and shared tips to familiarize me with the bohemian enclave of Miami. She suggested that I get lunch from the man who slow cooks ribs out of his truck on Grand Avenue, buy good weed at the Saturday market, and keep an eye out for the guy who bikes to Key Biscayne at noon everyday in a thong. *He sounds hard to miss.*

I got so caught up in conversation that I forgot to check my phone. Jon had texted me.

You really fucked us.

If I had accepted the third margarita that Alexandra offered, I might have responded more hatefully. Instead, I refrained and optimistically responded.

Everyone will be just fine!

He texted back.

Ross signed the agreement. It's at the front desk.

It was all over. Catherine's plan worked. I'd anticipated that Ross might "lawyer up", but he didn't. He knew he was wrong, and the threat of the news getting out scared him. In order to avoid any chance of running into my ex-colleagues in the hotel, I stayed at the pool until late afternoon when I adventured to the lobby to retrieve the document. The bellman handed me an envelope which included the signed agreement and a handwritten note from Ross.

Soluna, this won't be the last you hear from me. P.S. Tell the Cubans that I've smoked better Dominicans than the fucking sticks they gave us.

9

"*Mami*, Eighty six *papas fritas*," the bartender yelled.

I raised my hand, acknowledging the large man behind the bar. Several months ago, I'd communicate with co-workers with formal emails; now, I responded with a thumbs-up. I was wearing jean shorts, while serving pitchers of cheap beer and questionable seafood at a nearby waterfront dive bar.

After coming to the sobering realization that the roll out of The Miami Project would take longer than anticipated, I decided a short-term job was a practical strategy for my sanity, but mostly for my bank account. My Ivy League student loans weren't going to pay themselves.

More than four weeks had passed since I'd been able to confirm an upcoming in-person meeting with the Cubans. While their lack of urgency seemed to be a twisted psychological-warfare business tactic, it wasn't intentionally manipulative, but just cultural.

Since I was subjected to their slow, torturous timeline, my new job at Shotzee's allowed me to meet people in my new neighborhood and also not tap too much into my limited savings. While working at the bar, I tried not to share the specifics of Connect2Health, my recently-formed company. Even if I had taken the time to explain the business, no one would have cared. I quickly learned that if I asked questions about other people and seemed engaged with their lives, challenges, and struggles, they would be too preoccupied to ask anything about my life. I enjoyed my escape of not having to give answers or explain my untraditional, complicated story to anyone.

"Soluna, I hear you're out of french fries. How about sweet potato fries?" asked the guest with fiery red hair and an infectious smile.

"We got 'em, but it'll be like fifteen minutes," I responded. "Wait...why are you eating now? Don't you have a date soon?"

"I have two," he quickly piped back.

"Well, excuse me," I said, snapping my fingers to mimic his attitude.

"Remember Jared's golden rule of dating," he said, referring to himself in the third person. "Only drinks on the first date, never dinner."

"The more you know," I said.

The charmingly-immature man child spent Sunday afternoons on first dates with women he met on J-Date, a Jewish dating website. If the lovable schemers knew his upcoming date was very religious, he'd strategically wear a yarmulke. Recently, he recognized that his friends were going out to the club less and settled down, so he decided he should consider finding himself a wholesome woman. His "importing business" which I had yet to get the full run down on kept him traveling during weekdays, so he doubled down on his weekly routine of Sunday dates at Shotzee's.

Jared and I developed a clandestine code to use if his date needed an intervention. He'd flag me down and ask what oil the fries were cooked in. I'd respond with 'peanut oil', and he'd fake an allergic reaction. Jared had an allergic reaction every other weekend. As conniving as he was, I looked forward to working the Sunday afternoon shift. His presence was guaranteed entertainment, and he tipped well and in cash, always.

After dropping the check and waiting for a few of my tables to pay their bill, I scooted next to my favorite patron and accompanied him until his next date arrived. William, a fellow server, slithered up next to us and put his arm around me. He unapologetically interrupted, "*Mami*, I see you are off *mañana*. Want to cover my shift?"

"Sorry," I replied. "I can't. I'll be in out of town."

Jared inserted himself into the conversation. "She's going to *Habana*" he said in a dramatic Spanish accent.

"What the fuck are you doing there?" William asked combatively.

In an attempt to explain my work trip as simply as possible, I responded, "I have another job that requires me to travel to Cuba."

"So you're supporting the regime?"

"No! We're actually trying to put more money into Cuban people's pockets." The look on his face confirmed that I was in fact digging myself into a deeper whole. I should've just said Jared was joking and retreating into acting like the stereotype that William saw me as — a pumpkin latte-sipping blonde from the north.

"That's not how it works." He glared and crossed his arms. "You're making those bastards rich." He was referring to the Castro brothers and the select chosen ones in politics who led lifestyles that greatly contrasted with that of an average Cuban. "Damn, I thought you were cool," he said and stormed off, not sticking around to hear any details or further explanation.

I shook my head at Jared, who had remained silent throughout the entire exchange. I needed to be more cautious on whom I shared my business. I didn't want to alienate my Cuban-American co-workers. Everyone in Miami had an opinion about Cuba. Most Cuban-Americans were directly impacted by the mistreatment of friends and the sore wounds of family members being separated for generations. I should have known better to tell Jared to stay hush and not bring up my business trip to Havana.

A woman wearing a middle part and monogrammed necklace entered the restaurant. Jared chugged his beer and stood up. "Excuse me, my future wife is here." His final date for the evening had arrived.

10

The ice cream melted quicker than I could catch and lick the milky drips streaming down my fingers. Even though I was a mere thirty minute flight from Miami, the sun felt stronger, almost unfiltered, on my exposed skin. Rules dissipated and logic vanished. The exotic daily life of Havana played out around me. Despite the exhaustion-inducing midsummer heat, an energizing sense of freedom filled me from not being under the smothering oversight of Jon. With the firm, we'd taken a half dozen or so trips to the island, and each time I was subjected to following Ross around, serving as his translator due to his cultural incapacitation.

Chocolate dripped off the cone and smacked the ramshackle sidewalk. Ignoring the mess, I scrolled through the photos I had just taken of Coppelia, a factory-sized ice cream shop that looked like a once futuristic UFO landed in a public park. The unfathomable amount of dairy treats produced daily wasn't the only mind-boggling concept; so was the low price of the ice cream. Guests were presented with a decision: pay one USD to skip the line and receive a scoop immediately, or pay an amount in the Cuban Peso equivalent to thirty American cents but wait in line for at least an hour.

My recently-snapped photos showed the expansive, twisting line of hundreds of locals queued for their afternoon treat — capturing the ridiculousness. *Who'd wait an hour for a scoop of mediocre ice cream?* The idea of such a long line seemed unquantifiable and illogically perplexing that it needed to be experienced in-person.

Without thinking twice, I gladly paid the premium to enjoy the luxury of eating my late afternoon snack within minutes and avoiding the queue. *Wait in line for a full hour? No, thank you!* None of the locals opted for the quicker option, not only because they didn't have the money, but they had nothing else to do with their time. *Is this what the lines were like in Yugoslavia? Is this what my dad experienced growing up?* It seemed hard to imagine a world without the immediate gratification of drive-thru restaurants, pizza delivery, and vending machines.

In America, time is money. While in Cuba, time is time and money is just that, money.

I savored the last crunchy bite of my cone and pitied the people who had to wait a hour or so for theirs. Being born in America didn't just provide me with the privilege of possessing a different colored passport, but it gave me an entirely varied perspective and understanding of opportunity cost — the relation between time and money. I understood I had more productive things to do with my time, than just waiting in line. Unfortunately, the locals did not. Lines were a way of life in Cuba — a concept that illuminated my impatience.

My afternoon adventure led me to the *Malecón*, the five-mile promenade that hugs the decrepit, magical city. The welcoming sea breeze met my face as I escaped the cement-filled city and crossed the street to join the sea. Women in tight neon tube tops and men in equally-unfashionable rhinestone-studded shirts sauntered slowly. I settled into a large rock, allowing the waves to spray my overheated body. I sat staring off into the infinite distance, enjoying my first evening alone in Havana and allowing my scattered thoughts to settle. A silence crept, the type of silence that only Cuba could provide — no internet connectivity or sensory-overloaded news feeds, but distraction-less focus and clarity.

Just as the waves pumped and receded, my confidence in my ability to lead The Miami Project wavered. *What am I doing here? Will this actually work?* My eyes followed a group of graceful, gliding pelicans that were circling many darting fish below. The birds were taking turns swooping down like planes alternating times to land. While slow, they were strategic and took advantage of their unfair vantage and were monitoring the school of erratic fish right below the water's surface.

My uneasy feelings began to subside when I remembered the sterile boardrooms up north and how each colorless freezing morning I'd be woken to the sound of my alarm and filled with the feeling of internal dread of decades more of a lifeless, uninspiring day-to-day routine. I settled for that existence only for the pathetic hope of one day becoming a partner at a big name consulting firm.

A pelican swooped and pulled out a mouthful of fish, flapping off into the distance to enjoy its hard-earned bounty. I smiled, happy for the victorious bird and also having the realization that things which were so important to me, no longer mattered.

Despite being alone and championing a risky 'Hail Mary' project, there was nothing I'd rather be doing and nowhere I'd rather be.

11

The tumultuous rain dripped through the plastic awning and flooded the restaurant's patio. The hospitality industry in south Florida was weather-dependent. Thankfully, my dull morning shift was interrupted by Catherine calling. I answered, "*Hola!*"

"Hey lady!" said Catherine. Her peppy tone contrasted the depressing weather. "Any chance you want to join me in Medellín next week?"

"Huh?"

"I'm speaking at a conference and just discovered I have an extra pass," she said. "I'd like to introduce you to some investors."

There were five guests in the restaurant — three lonely drunk guys at the bar and a giggly Chinese couple taking selfies with their oversized mojitos. My chubby manager expressively waved his hands at me, signaling to me to get off my phone. I ignored him and replied to Catherine, "Sounds incredible! When should I plan to arrive?"

"Monday morning," she replied excitedly. "My assistant will send you the ticket and hotel confirmation."

Since Catherine and her husband were unable to conceive their own children, she enjoyed taking opportunities to be a motherly, nurturing figure to her younger associates. She was constantly sending me relevant news articles, introducing me to her network, and offering guidance on confusing situations of starting up a new business.

"So how's it going with the Cubans?" she probed.

"Slow."

"Well, we knew that," she laughed.

"You're right. I should say, 'slower than expected'. I met with Guido and Yandel yesterday at Hotel Nacional. I gave them each a microwave," I chuckled.

Each time I met with them, I'd bring a present. Just as I was learning how to run a business, I was learning how bribes worked. I brought my colleagues household items which were taken for granted in America, but luxurious to them.

"They loved it, and signed the contract in less than ten minutes. I spent most of the time listening to them as they insisted on pointing out a painting of every famous American who'd ever visited the hotel's bar."

"That's great!" she exclaimed. "Those guys are a good time."

"I think the actual meeting was so quick because I didn't need to translate." In the past, Ross had insisted that all of our conversations be held in English, which gave our negotiations an awkward flow. Ross was hypersensitive, believing that the Cubans were constantly talking negatively about him. His paranoia was warranted. *How could you live in Miami for decades and not retain enough Spanish to order his own meal?* Even the most stubborn of *gringos* in South Florida seemed to learn Spanish through osmosis.

"So what are the next steps?" asked Catherine.

"We'll receive a list of fifteen doctors. With that list, we can apply for Florida licensure. Guido estimated it should take about two months, but you know how that goes. I'm just frustrated that…"

Catherine interrupted me. "If it was easy, everyone would do it. Don't beat yourself up, Sol. You're doing the best possible job you can. I'm excited to see you soon."

A sleek, dark-grey yacht entered the restaurant's marina. Sappy Marc Anthony lyrics, remixed over the hard beat of a Trick Daddy song, blared from the vessel, causing an aggressive, reverberating wake.

"Sorry, I've got to go. I'm at work," I said as I slid open the refrigerator to see how many bottles of champagne were being chilled. "A guy who gave me a hundred-dollar tip yesterday just showed up. See you in Colombia!"

The man on the yacht began to violently wave for my attention and yelling "¡Mami! ¡Mami!" I was unsure which exact type of business he was involved in. It was a safe bet to say that this yacht owner was bribing the government in his native country to control an industry. My previously dull afternoon had taken a turn.

12

"Next!" called the US Border Patrol agent. I opened my passport to the picture page. The longer I looked at the man's face, the more I thought he resembled a neighbor from St. Louis. I shifted my eyes to peer down at his name badge. *Does Connor Lopez have a cousin in Miami?*

"Soluna?" asked the agent with penetrating brown eyes. I stayed staring at his badge.

"Yes, that's me," I responded, pointing at the name on my passport.

"What's up, neighbor?," he said, throwing aside his intimidating facade.

"Swan?" I stuttered. "You lived on Swan street?" Those were the only words I could spit out. It was the block that Connor and I both had grown up on. Even though he was a few years older than me, I remembered a tall, athletic neighbor catching my eye when he returned home for a week or two in the summer. He was well-known in our neighborhood as a prodigy from the local park district baseball league, who went on to play at the University of Texas. *From baseball to law enforcement, he looks good in uniforms.*

"Wow, you're the spitting image of your mom," he said, smiling.

"I hope that's a good thing," I responded.

"Don't play. You know that's a great thing," he chuckled. "We're grown now. You know your mom was one of the hottest moms in the neighborhood."

"Come on," I cringed. "She's still my mom!" My guy friends loved to tease me with comments about my mom. When the 'Stacy's Mom' song was popular, my friends cleverly remixed it to 'Soluna's Mom'.

Oblivious to the fact that we'd been holding up impatient travelers in the highly-coveted Global Entry line, we continued to laugh. In his professional protocol, he asked where I was coming from. When I answered 'Medellín', he joked that he may need to search me.

"Every other week we get tourists from Colombia who have bags of cocaine up them," said Connor. "You'd be surprised that people still smuggle on flights. It's so easy to ship drugs in the mail these days. It's FedEx's problem now, not ours."

"I promise I'm clean," I assured him. "I only brought back some chocolate and coffee."

"Sure," he said, and made air quotes with his fingers. "*Coffee.*"

"You must see some crazy things here. Any good stories?"

He laughed. "My job should be a reality show..." He continued to tell the story of how a Cuban man sedated and strapped two roosters to his inner thighs.

Although cockfighting was officially illegal in Miami-Dade county, the sport was popular in Hialeah, a Miami neighborhood that was more Cuban than the nation of Cuba itself. People in Cuba would breed and train champion cocks to sell in America. Just as the man lined up to get his passport stamped, one of the cocks woke up and began to rip the man's pants to shreds. Before the man was on American soil, he was pants-less, and a live animal had emerged.

I assured Connor that I had no cocaine on — or in — me, and certainly no cocks taped to my thighs, as I pointed down to my short flowing sundress. We laughed and both agreed it was great to see each other. He stamped my passport, and I was officially back in Miami — the city that offers the freedom of being abroad, but the protection of being in the United States of America.

The brief reminiscing of my old life served as a grounding reminder that my current life was worlds away from how I was raised. The next morning, I woke up to a text message from an unknown phone number with a 773 area code.

Tommy from down the block gave me your number. Dinner next week? We have to stick together down here ;)

13

"Sol," yelled a deep voice from the couch. "Why is everything in your Netflix suggestions about Pablo Escobar or Mexican cartels?"

"C'mon, Connor," I responded to the head and broad shoulders that peaked above the back of the couch in my living room. "You know that Connect2Health is just a front."

"Damn," he responded jokingly. "You fooled me." He continued to scroll while waiting for dinner to be served.

"But really, do you watch anything besides drug documentaries?"

I didn't respond, allowing him to answer the question for himself. I sauteed vegetables while trying to finish up work for the day. I was so engrossed in responding to an email that I didn't notice that the glaze on the salmon had begun to burn and catch fire. The fire alarm sounded. I hopped on the counter and used my laptop to fan the air around the blaring alarm. I erupted in a delirious squeal. The fillets of fish turned pitch black in the bubbling cast iron pan, and the thick smoke continued to fill my small home. Connor shot up from the couch and battled through the smoke. He located me by following my laughter.

After the fire alarm stopped, Connor and I found ourselves sitting on the ground, where we could avoid the oppressive-smelling smoke clouds. My uncontrolled laughter transitioned to an equally out-of-control cry. Connor knew that no words he said would console me, so he joined in on my laughter while wiping erratic tears from my face. He held me and pulled me closer to kiss my forehead.

Initially, I resisted him comforting me, but then I gave in to his embrace. He wasn't consoling me for my cooking mishap, but this was the first time I showed any obvious weakness in the months we'd spent together.

"I know you've got a lot going on," he said. "But I'd like to I treat you to a vacation."

I frowned. *He was right. I needed a break.*

He took my face that was transfixed on my phone's screen and redirected my focus to his face. "I thought Punta Cana would be fun. Neither of us have ever been, and it's a short flight."

"But..." I protested, though I wasn't sure what I was protesting.

He plucked my phone and slid it in his back pocket. "I think you should spend at least twenty-four hours away from your email. Doctor's orders."

"That's not fair."

"Trust me. We'll be having so much fun you'll forget all about your inbox." He playfully pulled me in. "I'll buy the tickets later this week."

"Thank you," I mumbled, as my head burrowed into his chest. I didn't want to face the mess on my stove — a sign of my blistering failure.

"So..." He kissed the top of my head. "I'll order a pizza."

14

"Two fish dips, a bucket of Kalik, and a bucket of Corona. Yeah?" I asked.

The table of eight middle-aged fishermen answered "*¡Si!*" in unison. I headed to the cash register to type in their order while checking my phone for the flight confirmation to Punta Cana. In the distance, I saw Jared come waltzing in for his Sunday afternoon ritual. I grabbed an ice-covered bottle of *Presidente* from the cooler and headed over to his table.

"Guess who's going to Punta Cana next week?" I boasted. I knew I'd get a reaction from Jared considering he'd been inviting me to his family's place in the Dominican Republic for the past month.

"You're joking?" sassed Jared. He took a swig of his beer.

"Connor surprised me with a trip. He says I work too much."

"Woah, so things are getting serious?"

"Mind your own business!" I said, playfully smacking his forearm.

"When are you going?" asked Jared.

"Next Thursday, coming back on Tuesday." I headed to the bar, as hordes of happy-hour guests were aggressively spilling in. For the next half hour, I buzzed between the tiki bar, tables, and the cash register. In a moment of peace after all the patrons were tended to, I returned to Jared.

"I hear you, bro. *¡Dalé! ¡Adios!*" he said, finishing up his phone conversation. He winked, thanking me for having noticed he was in need of a second beer. "That was my cousin Seth. He's a cardiologist that lives in the DR. Last month at my cousin's wedding, I was telling him about your work with the Cubans. If you're up for it, he'd like to meet you in Punta Cana."

"Ya, of course," I impulsively agreed.

"I think he wants to invest. He sees the potential of offering your services to the Dominicans in New York. He's like me," he bragged. "He knows a lot of people. He's a good guy to know."

"Thank you, Jared," I said, nodding my head impressed.

Did Jared just provide me with a valuable business contact? I figured his professional network only consisted of club promoters and strippers.

While the remainder of my shift dragged, the smell of tropical drinks and the feeling of the warm island breeze drew closer and closer.

15

Reentering the United States of America with Connor was the real-world's version of a Disney Fast Pass — no lines or questions. We were escorted to the desk where Connor's obnoxious co-worker Rafa greeted him. "*Oye*, damn bro! You got some sun!" joked the overweight agent. "Maybe you're really a beaner."

Connor received a lot of *mierda* at work because of his inability to speak Spanish despite his Mexican descent. The name tag on his bulletproof vest that read Agt. Lopez served as an invitation for Spanish-speaking visitors at Miami International Airport to speak to him in Spanish. He asserted that '*No hablo español*' was his most frequently-repeated sentence at work.

"What's good, Rafa?" Connor asked.

In an unprofessionally loud fashion, Rafa updated Connor about a drug bust that happened in the other terminal the previous night. "Bro, like, it was nuts..." While telling the story, he pressed several buttons on his computer without even asking where we were coming from. He was more focused on the story than about asking why we'd been out of the country.

Every night, Connor would tell me a variation of the same story. Some South American family pretended to be headed to Disney World, but they had cocaine stuffed in their children's Mickey and Minnie Mouse backpacks. I was unsure why Rafa was so animated about that particular story; I figured he may have stolen and used some of the confiscated contraband.

I zoned out Rafa and scanned the baggage claim belt in the distance, hoping to spot our suitcases. I had plans that evening to meet Jared at Sergio's, our favorite diner. We'd recently been hanging out outside Shotzee's to bounce business ideas off each other. We served as each other's unofficial support group for our entrepreneurial activities. He was adamant about meeting that night, because he had something urgent to run by me.

Rafa continued, "Bricks, bro. I'm talking the kinda shit you see in the movies..." Our passports were stamped, and we were back in the United States.

16

Jared had arrived before me and snagged our favorite go-to booth. As I sat down on the sticky plastic cushions, he dramatically declared, "A lot has happened since you've been away. I'd appreciate your feedback." Jared shuffled through his monogrammed Louis Vuitton backpack and pulled out a roll of toilet paper covered in glitter.

"Isn't that a health hazard?" I asked in astonishment. "You know, having the glitter stuck all up on your stuff?"

"Psssh! I don't care. The bitches at the club love it," he cackled. "We tested the product at LIV this weekend. We already got a thousand organic social shares and more than three million impressions from just those two nights...from toilet paper!" Jared referred to all things he sold as the *product*. He could make something as basic as toiletries sound exclusive and interesting.

"I leave the country for a weekend, and this is what you get yourself into," I joked.

"You're just jealous that you weren't able to wipe with glitter," smirked Jared. As crazy as Jared seemed, he was able to brand, market, and sell just about anything. Maybe it was my experience working in healthcare, but it just seemed absurd. I couldn't imagine sitting down to strategize about selling sparkly toilet paper, not when there were lives to be saved. *But who was I to judge? If there was a market for this sort of ridiculousness, it would be in Miami.*

"So how was Seth?" asked Jared. He gave me a look as if he was expecting me to spill some juicy, adulterous story that included me sleeping with his sexy half-Dominican cousin. "Did Connor get jealous?"

"Why are you always looking for trouble?" I asked. "Connor liked him! He learned a few Spanish words from him. They bonded over their gun collections." I shook my head in confusion. "I'm still not sure why a doctor needs a gun collection, but whatever..."

He began to grin. "Did Seth..."

"Oh my gosh!" I interjected. I reached into my purse and pulled out a package covered in 'Dora The Explorer' wrapping paper. "Before I forget, here's a present for Lucia."

Seth had given me a package to deliver to Jared. Jared and Seth's niece's birthday was coming up, and Seth wouldn't be able to attend the party in Boca Raton.

"Good work, kid!" Jared said, beginning to unwrap the present. I was confused as to why he was opening the gift from an uncle to a niece. I'd never met the girl, but she seemed like a sweet five-year-old who didn't deserve her presents being tampered with. Jared tore off the wrapping paper to find a board game called Pretty Pretty Princess. With complete disregard for Lucia, he ripped off the top of the box so the game's cheap plastic jewelry box was severed.

"What are you doing?" I exclaimed. "That's for Lucia!"

Jared began to smile from ear-to-ear, grinning like he was possessed. He didn't blink, quickly shifting his fixation between the torn-open gift and my face. *Why is he smirking at me like that?*

He reached into his designer backpack and pulled out a thick envelope, sliding it in my direction. "Here you go," he said. "You earned it."

"I earned it?" I asked. "What exactly did I do?"

Jared smirked, knowing my confusion was genuine. "I didn't want to tell you the actual value of the gift, because you would've freaked." My head tilted while he continued. "I wanted to prove to you that this work is in fact very simple." He reached into the board game and pulled out five little baggies of loose, dark red-tinted gems. "Also, I knew they weren't going to search you as long as Connor was with you."

"Are you kidding me?" I responded, slowly opening the thick envelope. "You used us. I wish I'd known."

"Well, congratulations," he declared unapologetically. "This was a test. You passed, and made yourself two stacks."

"What the hell are you talking about?" My eyes ping-ponged between his face and the envelope.

"Come on, Sol. I've been watching you ever since I met you at Shotzee's. You caught my eye because you're not like the other Miami girls," he said. "I knew you'd be worth pursuing to recruit for these types of jobs."

"You tricked me into smuggling! I could have gone to jail," I said, concerned. "And with Connor..."

He cut me off. "I'd like you to meet my uncle Youseff, and potentially work for our family's business. Well not for it, because you can't be on the books. See, we'd like to hire you as an independent contractor for transportation of..." He grinned and said, "High value assets."

I motioned for him to pass me the bag, and I examined what I'd unknowingly smuggled into the United States of America. I picked up a delicate finely-cut gem and held it up to the light to reveal its deep red hue. Despite having no concept of its monetary value, there was no denying its natural beauty.

"What the fuck, Jared?" I said as questions pulsed through my mind. *Could I have gone to jail? Was Connor suspicious?* "Is Seth even a doctor?"

"Yes, Seth is a cardiologist. But he also oversees our family's jewelry business in Santo Domingo. He's got contacts in Panama City, Mexico City, Havana, Medellín... all over Latin America." He twirled the straw in his coffee. "My family can't keep enough inventory in our stores in Boca and New York. We have access to discounted gems in Latin American cities, but we need to bring the inventory north. We'd prefer not to declare them, so we need someone like you."

"Someone like me?" I snapped back. "What does that mean?"

"Someone with no ties to Israel, no criminal record, and a legit reason to be traveling to these specific countries. Oh, and if you haven't noticed, you're *gringa!*"

"Thanks, I've noticed," I snidely replied. My curly blonde hair and light blue eyes didn't match the typical criminals pictured in the newspapers.

"Plus now you have an in with border patrol," he sneered playfully. "Connor has become the cherry on top of all this."

"Are you serious?"

"If you're interested, you'd get a third of whatever we save on the import tax. On three hundred grand of product, the savings would be eighteen grand. You'd get a third of that savings. Six thousand bucks... in cash."

I tilted my head, staring beyond Jared, and began to do simple arithmetic. *Six thousand dollars in cash is roughly two hundred hours at Shotzee's: almost thirty shifts.*

"All your travel and accommodation would be paid for. You'd never have to serve another table. You could use your newly-found free time for more important things."

He had a point. This was the easiest two thousand dollars I'd ever made. If I distanced myself from Connor, he'd never know. *It could work.*

"What happens if I get caught?" I asked with trepidation.

"I'm Jewish," he said sarcastically. "I've got four first and twelve second cousins who are attorneys."

"So why don't you do it?"

"I don't blend in," he said, never having made a truer statement. "Plus, I have a record. I got busted bringing ecstasy to Birthright."

"You're joking!"

Jared shrugged. "Do you want me to ask what *you* were up to in college?"

"Okay, point taken." I smiled and shook my head at him. "You never cease to surprise me." I took a deep cleansing breath and asked, "What would be the worst-case scenario?"

"You lose a jewel. You're burglarized." Jared said. "Um, I don't know...smuggling becomes a gateway drug, and you become addicted to a life of crime?" He laughed. "I guess you could always run away with the product."

"I wouldn't do that. I don't care for jewelry that much."

"I've noticed," he said, pointing to my left finger which had a dark green imprint from a cheap metal ring.

"Hey! What's that supposed to mean?" The smile drained from his face, and he gently reached one hand across the table. Taking my hand in his, he pressed it against the envelope full of cash. "Look, I'm offering you this opportunity because I trust you. You know the types of girls who are attracted to jewelry stores. Superficial, always taking selfies with the merchandise." He nodded towards me. "But you, I know you're focused and trustworthy. We've been looking for someone to fill this role for over a year. It'll ultimately be my uncle's decision, but you're the first person I feel confident introducing to him."

"This is a lot to take in," I inhaled. "That was extremely easy, but I don't want to get in any legal trouble. How'd I explain that to my parents?"

"I understand," Jared said gently.

"Or worse, what if I get locked up abroad?" Thoughts of a Third World jail cell raced through my mind. "Connor and I watched this show where these American students were locked up and never able to come back. They were forced to eat saltines for months. What would I do without these?" I said, forcing a small dramatic bite of an *empanada de pollo*.

"*¡Tranquila!* You won't get locked up! You have a privilege that not a lot of people have in Miami. You're *gringa*."

"I don't know..." I looked down at my meal which I immediately lost an appetite for. Feeling as if I had been on a rollercoaster since I sat in the booth, food was the last thing on my mind.

"You're starting to sound *loca*. You must be tired. Get some rest and buy yourself something nice. You deserve it." He put on his sunglasses and I saw my reflection in his frames with the money peeking out the corner of the envelope that lay in my hands.

"I feel weird taking your money," I confessed.

"You aren't taking it. You earned it!" Jared got up and threw a sparkle-covered hundred dollar bill on the table. "Pay the bill and keep the change. I'll talk to you *mañana*."

He scurried off into the night. Before he exited the diner, he was already on his phone, conversing about an upcoming event that he was co-hosting. His ability to jump from conversation-to-conversation and be fully present in each exchange was incredible. I barely felt present for our recent discussion, yet he was already on the phone planning his Saturday evening.

I flagged down the waitress and ordered, "*Dame un cortadito por favor.*" The caffeine was necessary for the long night of thinking ahead. There I sat in an diner with a flickering overhead light and a

Pretty Princess Game on the table next to my half-eaten *empanada*.

17

The rain pattered on the sky lights and the wind shook the palms outside my bedroom window. My sleepless, racing thoughts were harmonized by Connor's snoring. *Is this Youseff guy for real? What would Catherine think if she found out?*

Connor's warm breath on my neck served as the furnace for the runaway train of my thoughts. My eyes remained wide open, tethered to the ceiling. Instead of mulling over these questions all day until my meeting in Boca Raton, thankfully, I'd be occupying my time at Shotzee's. I'd agreed to cover a shift for my co-worker, Yennifer.

I owed her a huge favor. She had willingly picked up the tables that I was serving last week when Ross barged into Shotzee's. He and his pathetic crew had been assigned to my section on the patio. Once I saw the slobbish, arrogant man, I sprinted to the kitchen and sought refuge amongst the playful Bahamian kitchen staff.

While Yennifer was garnishing a salad, I pleaded to her that I needed to stay behind the kitchen door until that particular guest had left. I explained that I would do whatever to help prep the food, but I could not be seen in the restaurant. She had her share of vocal ex-boyfriends who came to the restaurant that she needed to dodge, so she understood. She covered my tables — no questions asked.

Since I opened up to her, she returned the favor and opened up to me. That evening she let me in on a secret of why she received so many "to-go" orders in cash. She was selling marijuana brownies and packaging them in take out containers to look as an order of hot wings. She asked if I wanted in on the action to make money on the side. I respectfully declined without even knowing if I would have a much more lucrative offer in the near future.

I couldn't have let Ross see me in my current situation — working at a Shotzee's. The snapshot of my life, a waitressing job, wasn't an accurate depiction of The Miami Project and its promise. I meant every word I'd said, that helping people was my motivation, but proving Ross, Jon, and the entire firm wrong was the fuel that kept me going.

Every shift after that, I kept a patrolling eye on the entrance, remaining perpetually anxious that

Ross would return to the watering hole within walking distance of his home.

Connor rolled in his sleep and faced me. I stared at his peaceful, resting face. *How am I going to keep this from him?*

18

A bright yellow car pulled up into the parking lot and honked twice. I stayed seated on the bench as I counted the pathetic amount of small bills I'd earned from a slow afternoon shift. The driver's window was open, revealing a dreadlocked man that offered a friendly wave. The backseat window rolled down, and I saw Jared's goofy smile. "Hey, *Gringa*, hop in! We have a long ride ahead of us." *Jared in a taxi? Jared would never pick me up in a taxi.*

I approached the car. Jared pushed the door open. I scooted in the back seat and asked, "No Uber?"

He was such an Uber loyalist. Since his speckled past had a way of keeping up with him, I assumed he had his license revoked from driving drunk.

Jared laughed. "Who needs Uber when you have my guy! Snoop, this is Soluna. Soluna, this is Snoop!"

"Hi, baby," the driver said in a high-pitched Jamaican accent.

"Snoop is Youseff's private driver. He'll give you rides to and from Boca. Snoop's the man!"

Years had passed since I'd sat in a traditional taxi cab. I remembered taxis having pictures identifying the drivers and other official licensing documents, but Snoop's car was different. The cab had a voodoo doll hanging around the rearview mirror and fluffy seat covers. There was no trace of any government regulation. Not only did the appearance of Snoop's car make it clear it wasn't a real taxi, but it reeked of weed.

"We'll miss rush-hour traffic," said Snoop. "We should be there in about sixty minutes or so."

Jared gave him a thumbs-up. "You still got that fire Damian Marley and Nas album?"

Snoop reached into his glove compartment. Several dominos, an empty bottle of Ting, and a half-smoked joint fell out. After he located and popped in the CD, he proceeded to light the newly-discovered joint and pass it back to Jared. Jared took a hit and offered it to me. I declined. I wanted to be fully coherent for the conversation that lay ahead.

An hour passed. We exited the highway and drove eastbound towards the sea. The distance between homes began to grow. We soon approached a gate. Jared instructed me that if I was asked to show identification, I should lie and tell the guard that I'd left my passport locked up at the hotel. Luckily, the guard didn't ask, but he gave Snoop a cordial head nod. We passed through the security stop unbothered.

Snoop kept an eye on the rearview mirror, enjoying the look on my awestruck face. He asked with a calm smile, "Ms. Soluna baby, you've ever seen homes this big? I think they're bigger than the White House." He wasn't wrong. The homes sat on multi-acre lots with guest homes, pools, and stables. I'd seen my fair share of large houses in Miami, but these homes weren't houses. These were compounds. *Where the hell am I?*

We pulled into the crescent-shaped driveway lined with foreign sports cars. Snoop stopped and exited the car, surrounded by a cloud of smoke. He ignored Jared's door and quickly walked around the car to open mine. "Thank you, Snoop," I said. My eyes swelled as I scanned the overwhelming Italian-style mansion. Snoop patted my back in a reassuring manner and said, "Good luck, baby. I'll wait for you right here."

Snoop's weed had a powerful smell, and Jared's continuous giggle confirmed that the strain was serious.

We approached the front door, where two life-sized stone lions protected the entrance. While I looked around for the doorbell, Jared mustered up some upper body strength and struck a large gong. The centering sound echoed through my body, helping to focus my attention on why we were here.

A petite woman opened the door. "*Mi amor!*" she said, spotting Jared. "*¿Cómo estás?*" She hugged Jared, and he began to rehash the events of his wild day. *Wait…Jared speaks Spanish? Will there be other surprises?*

"*¿Quién es ella?*" the woman questioned Jared, while smiling and pointing at me.

I responded in Spanish that I was a friend of Jared and here to meet Youseff. "*¡Hola! Soy una amiga de Jared. Me llamo Soluna. Vine a conocer a Youseff.*"

She was taken aback that I understood and responded.

"*Mucho gusto. Me llamo Mercedes,*" she replied and turned to Jared, hoping to learn that I was his girlfriend. "*¿Es tu novia?*"

"He wishes," I said, playfully nudging him in the stomach.

"*No,*" he replied, blushing. "*Mi pana.*"

"*¡Qué lástima!*" she said, shaking her head at Jared.

She turned and gave me a hug and then exclaimed, "*¡Qué linda!*"

Mercedes informed us that Youseff was finishing up dinner with his family, and he'd join us in the lounge in a moment. She led us through the foyer covered in museum-quality art, past the kitchen, to a dimly-lit room. Our shoes echoed on the ceramic tiles and thick glass panes that revealed a lower-level wine cellar. I let my body drop into the comfortable couch, allowing the thick leather to swallow me.

Peering through the full-length windows that overlooked the expansive backyard, I noticed several large, golden cages placed throughout the meticulously manicured grounds. My face must have displayed my confusion because Jared spoke. "My uncle collects exotic animals," he explained. "Lemurs, monkeys, and others I don't even know the names of. You know how some rich people like to hunt? Well, he and his friends like to collect injured animals and rehab them. He doesn't do much of the actual care himself, but he finances all of it."

It was hard to believe that this man was involved in some type of illegal activity, if he'd allow zookeepers to freely pass through his home. The

La Gringa

complex was as if Pablo Escobar's *Hacienda Nápoles* had uprooted and landed in present day Boca Raton.

Mercedes arrived with a bottle of wine, pouring out glasses for Jared and me. Moving to the back of the room, she opened up an antique record player. The lively sounds of a Spanish guitar brought the room to life. I sipped and peered over the thin glass, raising an eyebrow. I asked Jared a wordless question — 'What am I doing here?'

The heavy wooden door squeaked, and a man walked into the room. He had long brown hair and a well-groomed beard. Wearing a large smile, he came straight toward me. I stumbled to my feet. He threw his arms around me and exclaimed, *"¡La gringa!"*

I guess this nickname is sticking. The man gave me a dramatic kiss on the cheek. "Welcome to my home! I hope that Mercedes helped situate you with anything you may have needed."

"Yes, this Rioja is perfect," I responded.

He motioned for me to sit down, and pulled out a cigar from his front pocket to cut the tip. Once he lit it, he spoke. "It is a great honor to have you here. As I'm sure Jared was telling you, we've been waiting to have a conversation like this for a long time. A great opportunity is ahead, but as you can imagine," he paused to take a puff, "it will require the right type of discipline."

Youseff dove straight into it. I assumed there was going to be some type of small talk like him asking me what I did, or where I was from. But I soon realized he must have known all about me already through Jared. He explained that his family owned jewelry stores located throughout Latin America, and they needed to transfer gems from location-to-location, while evading the United States' import tax. He said the import tax wasn't that high, but with millions of dollars worth of jewelry it added up to a significant, unnecessary expense. Since the market was getting more and more competitive, he admitted it was becoming more difficult to increase their revenue with their traditional sources so they began seeking alternative, more creative sources for gems. He planned to decrease their operational costs to immediately increase their profit margin.

He suggested I begin with weekly trips to the Dominican Republic for the next month or two. I'd meet Seth in Santo Domingo on Tuesday evenings, and be given a package similar to what I'd brought back to Jared last week — an unassuming wrapped gift. The trips would become routine: leave Tuesday morning and return Wednesday evening. While the job could technically be completed in one day, he wanted to be cautious. "In and out" single-day trips were a red flag for the authorities. Youseff reminded me that I always needed to stick to the story that I was traveling for the purposes of my healthcare business. If I was asked by anyone in Santo Domingo, I should always say I was in town to meet with local doctors about expanding my United States-based company. Dominicans, he explained, loved to hear that American companies were expanding to their island.

Once I understood the logistics, we transitioned our preparation into role playing. We rehearsed in both English and Spanish, practicing my responses if I were questioned at the either the Dominican or American border. Luckily none of the questions were too challenging. Youseff constantly repeated, 'stick to your story', 'the less information you give, the better' and 'don't talk to strangers'.

"*¿Quieres más?*" Youseff asked, holding up the wine bottle.

"*Sí, ¡gracias!*" I responded. He smiled as he poured each of us another glass.

"Jared," said Youseff, switching gears. "I have great news! Chapo recently healed his broken leg, so he'll be able to go back to the zoo." Chapo, I assumed, must be one of Youseff's animals. He named all his pets after notorious drug traffickers or high-quality cigar brands. His recent transition in subject matter made me realize that Jared and he were indisputably related by blood. Never before had I met individuals who were able to so effortlessly and successfully jump from one topic to another.

"I'm so thankful," Youseff continued. "Soon he'll be able to play with his friends!"

Jared chuckled, "That's great news, but Lucia is going to miss him. No?"

"Yes, she will, but Lucia needs to understand that our backyard is not the best place for him. Chapo deserves to be with his animal friends."

"You got a point," said Jared.

Between the smell of the cigar collection, the exotic jungle beasts caged on the lawn, and the life-changing financial opportunity at stake, there was too much to take in. *A man that saves animals couldn't be too bad to work for, right?*

Youseff reached into his briefcase, pulling out an envelope and a colorful makeup bag. While he could've easily given me these items in a Ziploc bag, he instead presented them in an eccentric, thousand-dollar pouch. Extravagant was the most appropriate word to describe his appearance, actions, and overall aura. He opened the large manila envelope. Inside were several Benjamin Franklins, a healthy wad of multi-colored foreign bills, and a weathered passport.

"This is my cousin's ID." He held up the Israeli passport. "She runs our family office at the

Diamond Center in Tel Aviv. Please use it at the guard gate when you come to visit me. Never use your real name. The only issue is that she has brown eyes, so I have put a pair of reusable brown contacts in the bag. If you use this ID, make sure that you wear them. Hmm, what else?" he said, trying to focus. "I've included a cell phone that has my number, Snoop's, Seth's, and a few other numbers you may need."

I looked at the photo of Myra Levenfiche, hoping to encounter my Israeli doppelgänger, but unfortunately, I saw no resemblance. "But she doesn't look like me," I stated.

Youseff waved his hand at me. "It'll work," he responded, not allowing any time for any doubts. "If you accept, here is the roundtrip ticket for your first trip to Santo Domingo next week." He paused. *"¡Espera!"* He shot up and felt his pockets. "I'm forgetting something. I'll be right back." Youseff left the room, yelling *"¡Merce! ¡Merce! ¿Dónde está..."*

I turned to Jared and asked, "I thought there was going to be some type of test or vetting. So do I have the job?"

Jared smiled, amused at my continued discoveries. "Youseff sent a colleague to perform the final test earlier today. Do you remember the man who accidentally left you a hundred-and-fifty-dollar tip during lunch?"

"Yes, the poor guy had one too many of those Coconut Cartel drinks. The goof accidentally wrote a hundred and fifty instead of fifteen. Wait! How do..."

"That was your test. You could've easily charged him one-fifty since there was a paper trail. But you didn't. Youseff wanted to test if you'd be greedy and take advantage of the situation. The fact you charged him fifteen and not one hundred fifty proved to Youseff that you aren't looking to take money that isn't rightfully yours."

I threw a playful punch at Jared. "Are you serious? I thought that man was just a drunk that couldn't fill out the tip on the receipt. You're telling me that he was ordered by Youseff to get drunk and accidentally leave a hundred-and-fifty-dollar tip?"

"You got it. You see," he smirked. "Working for our family can be very fun." I racked my brain for other odd recent events to see if there were other previously unexplained Youseff-influenced situations.

Youseff returned to the den, holding a small box. "Everything you'll find in that makeup bag serves a purpose, but this here...well, this is more for luck." He handed me a gold-encrusted pendant necklace with a blue ocular charm.

"It's an evil eye. I give one to everyone who is important to our family. I know we just met, but Jared speaks very highly of you and cares for you a lot. A friend of Jared's is a friend of mine." He signaled for me to lift my hair. I gathered my thick, curly hair and held it up with my elbows spread wide. Youseff clasped the gift on my neck. "I wish you luck on this adventure and hope you wear this during your travels."

"Wow! Thank you very much. This is beautiful." At that moment, I didn't realize how much this evil-repelling, good luck trinket would be needed in the future.

"I've spoken enough," he sighed and leaned back in his throne-like chair. "Do you have any questions for me?"

I had many questions for him, but I remained silent. *Where is all his money from...the jewelry business? Is he involved in other shady businesses? Does he have other people smuggling for him? Or did they get caught?* And then I asked myself a question that trumped all the others questions. *Do I really want answers to these questions?*

"As of now, no." I refrained from asking, because I was unsure I was ready for the answers. "None that come to mind. I'm sure I'll have some soon."

"Take your time. Call me whenever you need to, from this phone," he said gathering the items into the bag. "Remember, Soluna and Youseff don't know each other. I'm keeping this distance to protect you. Our family is often under close watch. I want to keep you out of it."

Close watch, for what? I wondered.

He zipped the bag and handed it to me. "Send me a text this weekend. I'll share with you your hotel information when it gets closer."

"Sounds good," I nodded. I took the bag and held it in my lap. I looked up at Jared, hoping he'd have something to add, but he stared at me with a pride-filled smile.

Youseff interrupted our silent exchange. "Jared, want to stay the night?" he asked. "My meeting tomorrow got canceled. I figured we could take the boat out and dive. What do you think?"

"I'm down! I'll need to borrow some clothes though. You better not make me look like a *maricón*." I laughed, picturing Jared rocking a floral silk shirt, like the one Youseff was wearing.

Youseff stood up, signaling the conclusion of our meeting. "Soluna, I'm happy you met Snoop. He's been working with our family for years. Whenever you need him, he'll be there. Remember, always take an Uber to and from the airport. You need to always act as if you're traveling for your company. I don't think I need to say this, but I would be remiss if I don't," he added. "Your boyfriend can't know about this. The moment that he suspects anything is the moment this is all over."

"Understood," I said, pursing my lips. I began to plot the story I'd need to weave in order to keep Connor from becoming suspicious.

"Snoop will take you home now. It was great meeting you," he said, pecking me on the cheek. "I hope we have an opportunity to work together."

"Thank you for everything," I said, flustered. "The necklace is beautiful."

19

I pushed open the heavy front door and followed the well lit, weaving path to the taxi. Snoop was sitting on the hood of his car and staring up at the sky. He didn't turn, but sensed my arrival.

"You can actually see some stars when you head a little north," he said.

I looked up. With less light pollution, we could see more than we ever would be able to in illuminated Miami. Snoop hopped off the taxi and noticed what was hanging from my neck.

"So things went well?" he inferred by the gift that Youseff gave me.

"I think so…" I responded.

He grinned, amused at my shock. "Let's get you home."

Snoop opened the backseat's door and waited for me to scoot in before he shut it.

He put the key in the ignition but didn't turn it. Our eyes locked in the rearview mirror and he asked. "You understand how great of opportunity this is. Correct?"

I gulped and nodded. In that moment, we made a silent pact that it would be a conversation-less drive. He popped in a Shabba Ranks CD, and we merged south onto Interstate-95 and bobbed in sync to the music. Snoop understood that I was having a heated conversation in my head.

What are the consequences if I get caught? Would Youseff or Jared bail me out? Were plea deals a thing in Latin American countries? These questions I could have easily answered online, but I wasn't willing to put myself on a watch list from suspicious searches.

Fuck it. I didn't want to waste another hour working at Shotzee's, taking happy-hour orders from sloppy college kids and drunk boaters. Not when I could make thousands of dollars in an overnight trip. Transporting high-value assets one day a week would let me use the other six days of the week to build Connect2Health. While I couldn't tell Catherine explicitly about this money making opportunity, she'd be happy I wouldn't be wasting time working at the restaurant. *After all, she told me I need to value my time. Right?*

La Gringa

As we zoomed towards the Magic City's colorful, crane-speckled skyline, I rationalized my imminent illegal behavior. I figured everything in life was a risk. The Connect2Health deal with the Cubans was a risk. Smuggling for Youseff was a risk. The odds were in my favor. It was a calculated risk too rewarding to ignore. I snatched my phone from my purse and sent the restaurant industry's version of a resignation letter — a late night text message.

Hey Mauricio! Just got a new job in healthcare. It starts ASAP. I know it's slow there. Is giving 2 wks notice needed? Can you give my shifts to others?

Since it was halfway through the night shift, my boss had probably just railed his second line of cocaine. He responded immediately.

All good! Don't come tomorrow. Good luck & stop by for a drink once you settle into your new job.

My source of income just became a man that wears flamboyant clothes and rescues exotic animals. My family and friends from home would never understand. Luckily, I was sworn to secrecy so I didn't need to explain myself to anyone...not even Connor. He was the only person who would be just as excited that I was quitting Shotzee's. *How will I explain I could now afford to quit?* I couldn't tell him I'd now be smuggling jewels into the United States through the airport. *Hmm...since Connor had met Seth, I could tell him that Seth and some of his Dominican physician colleagues had decided to invest in Connect2Health.* I repeated the lie several times in my head, imagining how he'd perceive it. *"Their investment now allows me to pay myself a salary so I quit the restaurant."* It sounded like a very believable story.

Once we turned into my neighborhood, Snoop made a quick pit stop at the local liquor store. I followed Jared's recommendation to buy something nice for myself, and I proceeded to do something that I'd never done before — purchase a bottle of wine that cost fifty dollars. *Ballin'!*

20

Despite being months into my Tuesday morning routine, sleep still did not come easily. I'd force my eyes shut, but anticipation coursed through my veins, making it impossible to get a full night of sleep. Each Tuesday morning at 4:45am, my alarm clock would ring. Not for the purpose of waking me, but to shake me from the lucid dream-like state as I lay visualizing the day ahead.

Along with the alarm came an indecipherable mumble from the other side of the bed. "Shh! Back to sleep!" I'd say, and kiss his sleepy face. "See you tomorrow night." I'd hope that the next time I'd see him would be back in that bed and not at Customs.

I'd set the coffee machine and fetch an unmarked bag from the back of my closet that held Myra's outfit: a homely polyester skirt and unflattering sweater. Next, I'd pack my nondescript carry-on along with my laptop, Connect2Health pamphlets, pajamas, and toiletries - just enough for a quick twenty-four-hour trip.

Finally, I'd call a ride and be en route to Miami International Airport by 5:10am for the 6:20am flight. My early morning drivers were young men whose names always begin with Y. The once trendy names were a lasting gift from the Soviet Union to the tropical island. Yonathan, Yosbani, and Yoffrey would aggressively blast *Cubaton,* the Cuban-only reggaeton radio station, in order to stay awake after a long night of driving.

During our quick drive, we'd cruise by ambitious early-morning exercisers or dawn seekers returning from the club. It was the haunting time of day that could be considered either night or morning, depending on one's perspective.

After a month or so, I'd been able to recognize the majority of the characters who worked at the airport's curbside check-in desks. I noticed when they were freshly shaven, when they were assigned to a new post or when they came to work straight from a wild night, yet I never had any reason to interact with them. *Youseff's Rule #1: Never check a bag*.

As a blonde with a United States passport, I'd never been questioned, especially when leaving the United States. The least of my concerns was TSA, Transportation Security Association, the notoriously incompetent agency which was at the bottom of the totem pole of the government's authorities. My weekday routine was like a video game where each step increased in its level of difficulty. Level 1 was encountering a TSA agent: child's play. The final adrenaline-inducing level was carrying the gems through US Border Patrol and Customs. The evenings when Connor was working came with an increased risk and a rush, as if it were a bonus round in the video game. With each trip, my fear would dissipate and confidence would build. Every stamp on my passport was an accomplishment and a visual reminder of a job well done.

Happy to be taking advantage of the lasting perks previously expensed by the firm, I'd waltz to the Priority Boarding lane, still flaunting the queen-like status I'd earned from excessive business travel. The typical complimentary upgrade to first class would catapult me to the front of the plane and seat me next to middle-aged businessmen jaunting down to Santo Domingo. Most wore a smug look, as if the moment they touched down they'd be heading to a multi-million dollar, life-or-death negotiation.

While in the sky, I'd entertain myself by making up stories about the men sitting around me. Based on their dress, what was on their computer screen, and pre-flight pleasantries, I'd assess and assume where they'd be heading on *Hispaniola*. The unifying trait amongst the men was that they all owned watches that cost more than my car. They looked the same to me, but as Youseff told me. "Watches aren't just to tell time, but to tell other people about you."

Headphones stayed in my ears regardless if music was playing or not. They served as an excuse to avoid engaging in conversation. My clothes were bland. I wore nothing too eye-catching. The intention was to give my fellow travelers no reason to speak to me.

This money-making opportunity came at an ideal time. Catching early-morning flights served as an energizing distraction while communication from the Cubans lagged.

I'd arrive at Las Americas International Airport as Soluna and exit the airport as Myra. Once I cleared Customs, I'd head to the bathroom that lacked surveillance cameras at its entrance and switch into my more conservative identity. I'd pull my hair into a low ponytail, secure the wig, pop in the brown contacts, and fill my eyebrows in with a dark pencil. I'd change my dress to the long, shapeless black skirt and large, oversized sunglasses. A charismatic, chubby driver, arranged through Seth, was always there waiting for me with a sign: *Myra Levenfiche.*

The black car with tinted windows would take me to my hotel for the evening. My accommodations alternated between three business hotels, all of which had an upscale restaurant on the property. Seth would switch up the timing and location of our meetings, because he didn't want onlookers to suspect a routine. Myra and Seth would meet for dinner. *Señor Ramírez, una mesa para dos.*

I liked when he got caught up late at work and showed up in scrubs, a reminder that he was more than just a conductor of an illegal gem smuggling ring; he was a contributing citizen to society. Our conversations centered around the Miami Project, because he was excited to share any insight he could provide from his medical experience. He freely shared about his life, but it was difficult to decipher if it was all truthful or just arbitrary conversation that was acceptable to be overheard by the bartender. *Youseff's Rule #2: Every stranger is a threat.* At the end of our time together, he'd present me with a wrapped gift.

Unsure if it was wishful thinking, but he lingered around longer than the necessary amount of time required for a drop off. He enjoyed our weeknight rendezvouses - but we were business contacts. Just business contacts.

21

"*¿Sol - luna?*" asked the Dominican Customs Officer, confused by the origin of my name. "*No es un nombre dominicano, ¿no?*"

"*No, es gringo,*" I replied. "*Mis padres eran jipis.*" While my jet-setting mom may have considered herself one, in no definition of the word was my Old World father a hippie. Saying either of my parents was a pot-smoking flower child served as my typical dismissive response when people inquired about my name. Until I was able to do my own research, I'd believed my mom when she'd told me my name was derived from being born on an important lunar day. As a curious child, whenever I had access to a library or the internet, I researched my birth date — August 15, 1991 — to better understand the day's meaning. Despite my intense research, I'd never found anything significant about the date or the supposed event.

The inconsistency of my name's meaning defined my relationship with my mom during my teenage years. The more she withheld information, the more I assumed she was hiding something greater.

Despite her mistruths never being malicious, from a young age I sought and expected the truth from adults. One winter recess when I was home from college, I was flipping through the channels and heard the newscaster announce that the winter solstice would coincide with a full moon — a rare astrological event. It occurred to me that my birthday was in roughly nine months.

A few days later at Christmas dinner, surrounded by all my mom's relatives, I confronted her. "Mom, I know I was named after the night I was conceived, not the day I was born." That statement made for quite an awkward holiday meal with people who were more strangers than family to me.

From that day on, my mom knew never to feed me white lies, and she began to open up about her romance with my dad — a traditionally untouched topic. Talking about their relationship seemed to be cathartic for her, and it enabled me to fill in the gaps in my previously-disjointed family story.

My parents met when she was in Belgrade on a layover. Since she refused to eat airport food, she journeyed down the street from her hotel for a late-night meal. She ended up spending the whole night communicating by way of a Croatian-to-English paperback dictionary with a tall, dark man with light eyes. The next morning she didn't show up to her flight, because she'd accepted an invitation to spend the weekend at the captivating foreigner's home by the sea. The weekend turned into an inseparable summer, leading up to the first day of fall when my father proposed. Their plan was to marry the following year along the Adriatic Sea. But during the colder months, the war's violence peaked, and my mom soon discovered she was pregnant.

Her unplanned pregnancy was the reason she moved back to the United States — not just for better maternity care, but our overall safety. My dad's family owned a transportation company that became targeted by the Serbs. Some of their employees were kidnapped and killed on cross-country trips, so my parents agreed that I should be born and raised in the States until things smoothed over in his homeland.

If I hadn't been born, my mom would have stayed with her fiancé, but she chose her unborn child's safety over living with the love of her life. The distance strained their relationship, and the engagement was eventually called off. My dad stayed true to his promise of supporting and visiting his newborn American baby girl. Due to his involvement and sense of duty to his people, he stayed in Croatia until the turn of the millennium.

He constantly sent money and presents, and visited for important milestones - graduations and Catholic sacraments. I grew up always scared because my dad was away at war, but confused why he wasn't celebrated like the American soldiers. Once I understood the details of my parents' relationship, an overwhelming sense of appreciation and gratitude for my mom overtook me. Just as she learned to never to lie to me, I learned to never take her sacrifice or love for me for granted.

The boyish man continued to study my tattered passport, repeating my first name out loud. He looked up to me and said, *"Me encanta el nombre. Mi novia está embarazada de una niña. Voy a decirle el nombre."* I grinned because there may someday be a little girl running around Santo Domingo with my name, but mostly because I had one and a half million dollars worth of flawless, marquise cut diamonds shoved in my bra's underwire. That day was my most lucrative carry yet, and my name had served as a distraction.

22

"See," said Youseff, "this is the exact reason we need a woman on the team. I'd have never thought of this." Youseff fondled the foreign object as if he'd never held one. While he might have been happily married with children now, I was certain that with his swagger he'd handled many bras back in his day.

I smiled. "I mean, I figured they'd really need to suspect something from me if they were to take off my bra." Previously, I'd been hiding the gems in boxes of feminine products, an inconspicuous carrying vessel that no airport security wished to inspect. I felt wearing the gems on my person gave me more peace of mind, especially since the value of recent carries had begun to increase.

"You know who else did this?" asked Youseff.

"Did what?" I asked.

"Used bras to smuggle..."

"Jared?" I joked.

"No," he laughed. "Griselda Blanco." He continued to fiddle with it. "Before she became *La Madrina*, she ran a factory that made women's undergarments for smuggling cocaine."

"Now, those are big shoes to fill," I joked.

My creation impressed Youseff, further proving to him that I was taking mindful precautions to reduce our shared risk. Later that same evening, he presented me with a new assignment. As much as I enjoyed my late-night meetings with Seth in the Dominican Republic's capital, I was getting bored of the flights from Santo Domingo and back. Youseff sensed that I was ready for a new challenge, and I'd demonstrated that I could be trusted. To date, I had carried over ten million dollars' worth of product for him allowing me to make more two months than I had made during the entire last year. My boss proposed breaking the routine with a trip to Colombia.

23

I placed the key into my front door and pushed it open to find a visitor. Connor was on the couch, staring in my direction. He didn't greet me but remained silent.

"Hi, babe," I called.

"We need to talk," he said. *Is he breaking up with me?* I scanned the kitchen countertop to see a cereal box and his lactose-free milk.

"Cereal?" I nervously questioned. Connor was a very regimented eater so a bowl of sugar for breakfast was out of character.

"Are you dealing?" he asked. *Shit! He noticed what's between the cereal box and the plastic bag liner.*

"What?" I swallowed and inhaled slowly to grant myself some time to figure how to react.

"Drugs?" he asked. "Are you dealing drugs?"

"When would I have the time to do that?" I laughed and made my way to the kitchen to pour myself a glass of water. "Those are old tips from Shotzee's," I responded. *Does he know about Yennifer? I thought I told him I declined her offer to join her in selling weed.*

"Ten thousand dollars in tips?" His blood shot eyes from working the nightshift didn't blink. "Those are blue-faced, banded hundred dollar bills. Don't bullshit me."

I began to chug using my thirst as an excuse not to answer, but his eyes continued to press. He knew I was lying.

"See, my dad he told me not to trust banks. His money got seized when he was younger by the communists." I acted embarrassed hoping my self-deprecation would get me out of questions. "I guess it's a weird quirk I learned from him, but I always keep a decent amount of cash hidden."

"Why didn't you ever mention it to me?"

"It's kind of pathetic. I figured you'd think I was silly."

"Silly is being convinced that my girlfriend is a drug dealer."

"Me? Come on," I smirked. "Even if I were, what would be that bad?" As my nerves diminished, his concern grew. I leaned for a kiss. He pulled away.

"I hate people who are drug dealers." His eyes narrowed.

"I know you probably see a lot of shit at work," I said trying to understand his visceral reaction.

"No, Sol," he stuttered. "I've never told anyone but," I took his hand. "My mom is an addict." He looked down.

"Your mom?" The image of the cheery woman across the street from my childhood home popped in my head. She was known for making delicious chocolate chip cookies and always hosting epic barbecues. *She can't be an addict?*

"So, my mom is not my birth mother," he said. My eyes widened. "Before my dad met Mary Pat, he had me with another woman."

It made sense. He was taller and had a different facial structure than his younger siblings. *Was it obvious and I was an oblivious child? Does my mom know this? Is this a neighborhood-wide secret?*

His eyes welled up as he continued to explain. The week after he committed to a full-ride baseball scholarship was a whirlwind. He received a lot of local press for signing such an impressive scholarship. I even remember gossiping neighbors saying that he may go straight to the Major League. He explained that the joy-filled week came to an end when a raggedy woman was waiting outside his high school in the parking lot. She kept going up to the students asking for Connor.

He continued, "She looked crazy. I'm talking clinically insane. I had no idea why this possessed woman kept saying 'Remember me?' She wasn't even forming coherent sentences."

I didn't speak. I kept rubbing his shoulder encouraging him.

"I tried to shoo her off but right before I closed the door to my car in order to escape her, she said 'Do you still have the birthmark on the back of your right upper thigh.' That's when I froze because I knew she could actually be my mom."

"Wow!"

"Now I understand why my dad kept this from me but back then I didn't speak to him for a month. I was pissed. He understood that I wanted to get to know my real mom, but he begged me never, ever give her cash." Connor breathed deeply. "I began piecing things together. Every Saturday morning, I'd catch my dad reading the obituaries section of the local paper. I thought it was weird, but I never asked why. Now a lot more makes sense. He was checking to see if she had overdosed."

Up until that day, I thought the family across the street was perfect; a perfect mom, perfect dad, perfect kids, but their story was anything from perfect.

"When I was home for a weekend during the final semester of my senior year, I met with her for lunch. I was updating her on my plans and letting her know that I wasn't going to pursue playing professional ball because of my recurring knee injury. It was tough to process my dream wasn't going to become a reality, but I remember being so proud to tell her about the job offers I had received in Houston. She didn't care." He shook his head. "After we finished eating, I went to the bathroom. When I returned, she was gone. She stole my car keys off the table."

"Oh my god," I said.

"She ended up totaling my car later that night. I haven't spoken to her since I pressed charges. See Sol," he slowed down his pace. "Once she realized I wasn't going to be the loaded professional athlete that she always hoped for, she abandoned me…again."

My hand rubbed his buzzed hair. While admiring the bravery in his vulnerability, a sense of jealousy crept in. He had revealed something he had been holding in for so long; it must have felt good.

"So this is why I don't drink," he sighed. "Apparently, addiction is in my genes." I wrongfully assumed he didn't drink because he cared about his appearance, mostly vanity reasons. *Why'd I never ask? What other assumptions have I made?* "So this whole experience is why I want to be on the drug task force at CBP," his voice trembled. "Drugs don't affect just the users but can destroy families…"

My hands carefully held his flushed face. "Rest assured, I'm not a drug dealer." I looked him directly in the eyes. "Thank you for telling me. I had no idea."

The water in his eyes hit capacity. A heavy tear rolled down his cheek. I didn't know he was capable of crying. He was always poised and in control of his emotions. I threw my arms around his large muscular frame and sat my chin on his shoulder. I looked up to see the stack of money next to the sink. *I need to find a better hiding spot.*

24

The sound of sizzling steak overpowered my growling stomach. While I waited for an early evening meeting in Medellín's bustling business district, I marveled at the green foliage surrounding the restaurant's courtyard. Before my recent travels to Colombia, I had wrongfully misjudged the notorious city and was surprised to find a lush jungle peacefully woven throughout the enormous valley.

A man approached the table, dressed in a slightly too small polo with tight jeans and covered in a film of dewy sweat. His attention turned to me. "¿*Eres Myra?*" he questioned.

"*Si*," I confirmed. *Why does Youseff think this disguise is necessary?* My unattractive appearance seemed to draw more attention than it avoided. *Maybe I'm being dramatic. He knows what he's doing.* The man looked at my outfit — that I wouldn't be caught dead wearing if I wasn't acting as Myra — and shook his head. I was well aware that I didn't look cute, but I was offended by this man's rudeness to Myra. I felt like I needed to defend her. *Dude, don't be a dick!* Like most Colombian men, he didn't know how to respond to Myra's orthodox garb. He was accustomed to women in tight-fitting clothes who flaunted every God-given or doctor-enhanced curve on their body.

He quickly sat down, flagged the server, and ordered a double espresso. After he lit a cigarette, he confessed in a thick accent, "Wow, you're a woman."

"*Sí,*" I responded, unsure if I was confirming his statement or answering a question.

"*Pero* this is dangerous," he looked around. "Why'd Bling send you?"

"Bling?" I asked. "*¿Quién es Bling?*"

"*El Judío,*" he replied. "Youseff." His mouth continued to move, but the hunger pangs made it difficult to concentrate. After several minutes of shooting a stern, disinterested stare in his direction, I abruptly zoned back in when he smacked the table with his hands adorned in gold rings.

"*Recuerda no confiaren nadie,*" he repeated. "*¡No confiar en nadie!*" His never-ending warning soon transitioned to a nostalgic soliloquy educating me on Youseff's early career. He described my boss as the cocky hotshot who came to Medellín during the Emerald Wars, a period of severe violence due to exploitation of the country's valuable natural resource. The Colombians laughed him off at first.

But once he proved he was able to sell so many jewels — enabling them to launder their money — he had the attention of Colombia's most powerful families. Youseff was able to sell such large amounts of emeralds and diamonds that all the narco traffickers used him as a strategic partner in the United States and abroad. He helped the Colombians sell their precious emeralds across the world from London to Paris and even Tel Aviv. Jewelry was great way to launder their money and not rely on their Latin American currency which was subject to extreme fluctuation.

He kept referring to Youseff as Bling — a nickname that I was not yet privy to. Supposedly, during the peak of his Latin American conquests, Youseff was responsible for influencing Miami's budding scene to be the flashy, jewelry-focused culture along the time of the rise of Rick Ross and DJ Khaled. Almost every rapper's chain in a Miami-filmed music video in 2006 was sourced by Youseff. While these stories dated Youseff, his youthful energy and young children had me deceived. I always assumed that he was in his late thirties like his cousin, but if I did the math correctly from the intel of these new stories, he must be in his mid-forties. *Good for him! I need to ask him what he does for his skincare routine.*

The finicky, no-named man across from me continued puffing smoke in my face. My appetite disappeared. Frankly, we both aimed to end our meeting as quickly as possible. He didn't want to look at my unattractive appearance, and I wanted to remove myself from both the uncomfortable, judgmental stares and itchy skirt. Once he realized I was no longer listening, he asked me the first question of the night after confirming my name, "*¿Fumas?*"

"*No*," I responded.

He smacked the table. "*¡En Medellín, tú fumas!*" he declared, nudging a pack of cigarettes against my arm. He laid down a colorful bill to cover the cost of his coffee, and fled without offering a proper goodbye. On his hustle out of the restaurant, he collided with a man who looked as if Gianni Versace returned from the dead. He wore a flashy belt buckle, slick gelled-back hair, and loose-fitting silk shirt.

"*¡Cuidado, mariposa!*" my contact warned, puffing his shoulders. The eye-catching man brushed off the insult and scanned the dining room with his shifty eyes. An unsettling feeling crept. The Colombia assignment were different because Seth was not around. *Not only do I not know anyone in Colombia, I don't know anyone in the entire South American continent.* I signaled for the check in hopes of retreating to my comforting hotel as soon as possible. I slid the cigarette package into my purse.

25

My eyes stared at my laptop's welcome screen, hoping to encounter the message that I'd been waiting on for months. That evening in Medellín was the hundredth time that I'd logged in to my email, expecting to receive the much-anticipated list of doctors. The absence of a list was holding up the entire rollout of the Miami Project. While I had the attention of the local pharmacies as distribution partners, I needed to manage their expectations for the rollout of the services since the Cubans were dragging. Previously, I'd be excited when refreshing my inbox, but now I was frustrated and annoyed at the delay. In my optimistic naiveté, I'd believed the timelines presented by my communist colleagues.

I took my first sip of wine to soothe the impending disappointment, but then rubbed my eyes to confirm what I'd seen was correct. Sandwiched between dozens of emails was one with the subject: *Los Medicos.* I gulped and clicked. *Dr. Ana Morales, Dr. Guido Alvarez...*

Like when the safety strap becomes fastened on a rollercoaster, my stomach sunk. The ride was about to begin. The Miami Project was no longer theory; it was a business, and now was the time for its roll out. *About time!* I snatched my phone, ignoring the inevitable international fees, and called Catherine. She answered. "Guess who got the list?" I gloated.

"Finally!" she cheered.

"I cannot believe it's actually happening!" I said, rereading the list to myself. I imagined each doctor's unique appearance and personality to fit their names. *Are they young or old? Do they have family in America? Do they support Castro?*

"Where are you?"

"Uhhhh," I paused looking around. "A Colombian restaurant." I didn't want to lie or explain why I was out of the country.

"Soluna, give me a second," she pleaded amongst many voices in the background. She dramatically raised her voice, "this sounds VERY urgent!"

I knew what she was doing, but I hoped the people around her didn't. She was using my call as an excuse to escape a soul-sucking midweek meal with clients. *I don't miss those!*

"No worries," I said. While waiting for her to return, I scanned the lobby. My eyes locked with a recognizable face across the room. He immediately disengaged and pretended to be reading the menu which was upside down. *Why is he here? What are the chances he was at the restaurant and now the hotel?* My eyes returned to the screen. *Don't be paranoid. Focus on the list!*

Catherine returned to the line. "Forward me the email, please."

Excitement pulsed through the phone. "Let's draft the application so you can send it off tomorrow."

For the next hour, I took advantage of my surge of energy and the strong WiFi connection to complete the Florida licensure application so the lawyers could give their expensive blessing in the morning. Time was of the essence and for the first time, the ball was in my court to push its progress along. Despite visualizing and rehearsing for this moment over the past months, I never imagined it would come to fruition in the lobby of a hotel in Medellín.

The euphoria soon became overshadowed by my continued focus on the man who would look my way every time I diverted my attention from my screen. Everyone had emptied out of the bar, and it was just us two. He was clearly not waiting for anyone, but me. While many well-endowed women passed through, the man's eyes kept wandering to the man at the front desk. If my stalker's outfit and the way he carried himself were any indication, I knew he wasn't sticking around to ask me on a date. I felt like his prey, and he was ready to pounce. *What does he want?*

I walked to the lobby and greeted the hotel employee who was pecking furiously at his keyboard. "*Hola*," I said.

He abandoned his typing and said, "*Hola!*" Like most people in Latin America, once he saw my appearance, he switched to English. "How can I help you?"

"Question for you..." I paused and offered the first stereotypical question that a Pablo Escobar-obsessed American tourist would ask. "Do you have a driver who could bring me to *La Catedral*?"

I glanced back at the bar to ensure my stalker was out of earshot. He was staring me down. I propped my shoulders and turned my back so he couldn't read my lips.

His perfectly-plucked eyebrows bobbed as he enthusiastically responded. He took out his cell phone to show me the social media profile of a tour company that he highly recommended.

"Will you be around tonight if I have any more questions?" I asked the man who'd be the unlikely protagonist in my brewing escape plan.

"No, sorry," he said. "I get off at nine."

"Perfect," I stuttered. "I mean, thank you."

Across the hallway, a family exited the elevator. I darted and squeezed my body between the closing doors. Just before they shut, I looked back to see if the man in the bar earlier was watching me; he was. I pressed '6' and ascended.

I exited on the sixth floor, but I ran up the stairs two levels, double locked the door and dragged the sofa chair to barricade the only entrance. I darted to the window which overlooked the hotel's entrance. I lifted the curtain, allowing only my eyes to peep through. My stalker was departing the lobby in a manic walk to a grey car that sat between the hotel's entrance and the city street. He unlocked the car from the passenger's door and reached into the glove compartment. He grabbed an object and shoved it in his belt behind his back. *Fuck! He's strapped.*

I knew nothing about the man I received the emeralds from and even less about the city. *How will I get to the airport? Did the sketchy contact set me up?* My imagination ran wild. *Will he follow me to the airport? Will this become a car chase? Will he try to run my taxi off some winding, countryside highway?*

I filled the haunting silence with a low budget, trashy Mexican *telenovela* and paced from the door to the window, occasionally stopping to purposelessly gather my few belongings for no other reason than to keep my hands busy.

I sat on my bed, staring at the daylight fading against the monstrous green mountains that hugged the city. Heat lightning danced in the distance, serving as an ominous, claustrophobic reminder that I was trapped.

Youseff sent his typical evening text.

¿Todo bien?

I lied and didn't alert Youseff, because there was nothing he could do, being a thousand miles away. Plus, there was still a chance that I'd made up all the concern my head, and I was overreacting. I didn't want my boss to lose faith in me.

The nighttime hours passed excruciatingly slowly. It was almost midnight and the boxed-shaped truck with a yellow and navy *Envigado* license plate was still lurking outside the hotel. A steady red ember burned outside its window. There he was, my stalker from the bar, his face illuminated from the constant glow of his phone screen. From the hungry way he had been eyeing the attractive men in the bar, I inferred he was now occupying his time by being on a dating app. His attention was consumed.

While my sleep-deprived body wanted to close my eyes, my paranoid mind was in overdrive, imagining every worst-case scenario. I kept swiping on my phone, hoping I was right. I had downloaded every gay dating app I knew of. With each flamboyant profile that appeared on my screen, I swiped them away.

There he was... Hector Luis, 36. I swiped yes and bit my lip. Watching him out of the window, nervously. *Please respond, please respond, please...*

My phone buzzed. *Match.*

My plan was in action. I sent the first message. There was no time to be bashful. I wanted to escape the hotel and get to the airport as soon as possible. I sent an overtly-forward message that I'd never dare send if it were my own personal account.

Was it you I saw sitting at the bar early? Why did you not stop to say hi? ;)

The disguise would be easy, but executing the decoy would be a little more complicated. I phoned housekeeping for a toothbrush. While waiting for the delivery to arrive, I checked the dating app to see if I had received a response. Earlier that evening I had made a fake dating app profile for Javier, the hotel employee that kept catching my stalker's eyes. I gathered photos from his public social media profile. In addition to the photos, I took a few creative liberties on his profile. Since I had become a serial smuggler, I figure adding identity theft to my rap sheet wasn't too far-fetched.

My strategizing of the next flirty, luring message to send was interrupted by a knock at the door. The maid handed me a toothbrush. "Grassy-ass!" I responded in an extreme American accent, hoping that if I shed my Spanish speaking abilities, I could ride out the privilege of being a rare *gringa* in Colombia to get what I was about to request next.

"*Con gusto,*" she replied.

"My suitcase was stolen and I have a flight early this morning," I continued. "Since all the shops are closed, can I buy one of your uniforms?"

She looked at me strangely. Realizing that she didn't speak English, I immediately responded, "*Puedo pagarte.*" I flashed three hundred thousand Colombian pesos, the equivalent of one hundred dollars and repeated my request in Spanish. She rightfully knew that there was no stolen suitcase, but she was not willing to ask questions. The money that she was about to receive could pay a few months of rent.

"*Si, señorita,*" she nodded. "*Dame un momentito.*"

"*Gracias, paisa,*" I said. Next, I called the front desk to let them know that I may be expecting a guest and to please allow him to check in.

Within minutes, there was another knock at the door, quicker than expected. A smiley, soon-to-be wealthy maid handed me one of her uniforms. I reached into my pocket and pulled out the agreed-upon wad of pesos.

I quickly closed the door and sent a message.

I have a break. Want to fool around in a guest room?

I slipped out of the towel and into the loose-fitting, starchy uniform. While pulling my thick hair in a low braid, I peeped through the bottom of the shade to watch if the man was prompted by my recent suggestive message. He exited his car and went around to the trunk in a stimulated, giddy manner to spray himself with cologne. *This dude is so desperate.*

The final part of the decoy was about to be in action. I sent a message.

Check in for room 812. A key is waiting for you. ;)

He locked his car and walked towards the lobby. I fiddled with the radio, scanning until I found sultry Spanish guitar that seemed fitting for a raunchy rendezvous.

I swung the security bolt leaving the door cracked open and sprinted for the stairwell. I allowed my legs to tumble down the dirty, industrial staircase. The exit opened to a dumpster-filled alley. I ran to the

street, turned the corner, and heaved my body into
the nearest idling taxi.

"*El aeropuerto.*"

The back seat of the car served as my
changing room. I needed to return to my actual
identity, in preparation to pass through airport
security. Each time I stripped a reminder of Myra
from my person, I encouraged the driver to increase
his speed by throwing bills at him.

26

She doesn't deserve this. Catherine put all her trust in me. I let her down.

My thin elastic pants were no barrier for the ice cold metal chair in the center of the unmarked room. I'd been detained for hours and developed an itch on my lower back that I couldn't reach despite constant squirming. The handcuffs and leg clamps were too restricting. Goosebumps stood erect on my forearms like watch dogs awaiting the next threat.

Ugh, and my mom...she's going to freak out. I don't even want to think about my dad. He'll for sure be on the next flight to Medellín, and probably use some outdated Yugoslavian scare tactics on the police. I guarantee he'll call his buddies to see if they have any connections in local government here. And Connor... he's going to think I used him.

All my belongings were spread, and my suitcase laid open, having been torn through. The cinder block walls held no clocks or windows. My reflection was the only thing I could see in the double-sided mirror. I assumed the authorities that dragged me into the holding cell were on the other side, scrutinizing my every move.

The only incriminating possessions were the dozens of thinly-cut five carat emeralds collecting heat against my chest. Right after they pulled me from the Passport Control line, they conducted a thorough search of my bag, but not my body.

Medellín wasn't worth it. I should've just stuck to my previous routine. Despite the internal crumbling taking place, I stayed superficially unbothered.

Did Hector tip them off because he didn't get what he came for? Is the sweaty emerald dealer working for the government?

The metal table rattled with a slam of the door. A stern, emotionless woman entered. Her appearance proved to be more intimidating than her tone. "We were alerted that a Jewish-American citizen is leaving Medellín and carrying illegally sourced emeralds. She was described around your age and supposedly arrived at the airport at the same time you did."

The woman reached in her back pocket and pulled out blue latex gloves to reinspect my belongings. I looked in the mirror to critique my body language. I doubled down on asserting my annoyance. If I was truly innocent, I figured by now I should be pissed for being wrongfully detained for so long and missing my original flight.

"You have the wrong person," I said. "I was here for work. And Jewish?" I clenched one of the two necklaces that hung from my neck. The gold cross was a gift from my Croatian grandmother that was blessed in Medjugorje. "Do I look Jewish?"

The woman interrogating me seemed to sense the accusation was absurd. In between rummaging through my belongings, she slipped in a few smiles, expressing her pity but need to adhere to protocol.

"Please, I don't want to miss the next flight," I said. My flight took off hours ago, I knew there were only a limited amount of direct flights to Miami.

Myra's belongings lay in a garbage can off the side of the highway around a mile from the airport. Myra's actual ID sat comfortably in the center console of Snoop's taxi. From the guidance of Youseff, I used a digital ID when I checked into hotels as Myra. He instructed me to 'make up some bullshit that Israeli IDs are all digital'. He was correct. Latin American hotels never questioned it.

I refrained from asking the Colombian authorities if I could call a lawyer because I figured that might sound like I was culpable. *Even if I did get to call a lawyer...who would I call?* I'd never even gotten a traffic ticket before.

She turned to me, giving a sympathetic look. *Fuck! I hope that's not a preemptive apology for having to do a cavity search. If they didn't do a proper pat down, I doubt they'd dive into such an invasive search. Right?*

In preparation for Colombia, Youseff explained there may be a very rare emergency situation where I'd need to use the condoms in the make up bag and insert the gems into me. This tactic of concealing contraband was common in the eighties before body scanners. This strategy made women more attractive mules, given that they're more anatomically advantaged to smuggle with twice the carrying compartments.

The door blasted open. The woman's look towards me was interrupted. *Thank god!* A man in a suit entered, holding a boxy cell phone.

"Señorita, es para usted," he told me.

The woman was surprised and asked, *"¿Quién es?"*

"El gobierno," he responded nervously.

My hands were restrained, so he held the phone to my ear.

"¿Hola?" I said, unsure who'd be on the other end of the line.

"Good afternoon, Soluna." said a familiar voice. "I'm calling on behalf of Ambassador Ruiz." I exhaled in relief. "Listen up," said Youseff. The phrase was his way of telling me to 'kindly shut up.' I grinned.

He continued to explain that he was communicating directly with the Colombian government. "You understand that you and your business are an asset to the United States so this is a top priority to get this resolved. This situation makes Colombia look bad. They've been doing everything to improve their reputation. They're attempting to increase their trust for global trade partners."

Youseff's theatrical performance was because he assumed he was on speaker phone. I remained silent, not wanting to speak over my boss. "You'll be released soon. Don't be afraid to have an attitude. You shouldn't have been detained."

"Thank you, sir."

"Soluna, remember," the comforting voice said. "I always have an eye on you..."

The guard released my handcuffs an hour or so after Youseff had called. I clenched the circumference of my wrists and rubbed them to rid them from the red marks. They told me they'd arranged my return on another flight. *But there are no evening flights to Miami. Will I have a layover?* I remained silent, being too afraid to ask.

After I reorganized my bag, a man in a bulky, green, bullet-proof uniform led me outside, to an armored black SUV. The seats in the back row faced each other. Even though I was supposedly released, the stoic man kept his monitoring eyes on me the entire ride across the runway. We drove past the final commercial airplane. They kept getting smaller and smaller. *Where are they taking me?*

We made a quick turn to reveal an illuminated hangar with a small jet. He spoke. "Miss, this is your plane." *You've got to be kidding me?* I had gone from being locked up in an interrogation room to being escorted to a private jet within an hour. I felt like an international criminal being extradited or a prisoner of war returned to their country as a political favor.

I exited the vehicle while the man gave my suitcase to the flight attendant. I was presented with a glass of champagne before I stepped up on the stairs. I moved slowly, as I had never been on a private jet before and I was unsure of the proper etiquette. A middle-aged man sat reading The Economist with his legs crossed and several buttons of his suit's shirt undone. He smiled and returned his gaze to the magazine. His greeting was a courteous warning to not engage; the same type of unengaged greeting I wore when dressed as Myra.

I replied with a trailing "*Hola…*" My head swiveled, marveling at the jet's luxurious interior. The large leather chairs had monogrammed initials surrounding a regal crowned bee, presumably a family crest. *Who is this man?* My travel companion appeared to be unwinding so I respected his silence. *It is probably his plane after all.*

27

Our smooth, peaceful flight glided into Miami-Opa Locka Executive Airport just before midnight. With vintage French wine and classical music filling the cabin, I savored the weightless, worry-free feeling I assumed that the mega-rich enjoy every day.

We disembarked the plane, and a U.S. Border and Customs agent with a five-o'clock shadow was waiting for me. "Why did you leave the country?" The emptiness in his tone suggested that he'd received tenure and was granted the easy shift at this private airport.

"Business," I responded. By providing a vague, generic answer, I hoped he wouldn't prod further. He didn't.

Snoop and Youseff were at the far end of the parking lot as if waiting to pick up their child from school. Youseff was nervously pacing back and forth while Snoop had the hood lifted and was fiddling with the engine. When the boss saw me pass through the exit, he shot his hand up in a "V" formation declaring victory and jogged towards me. I didn't have the energy to meet him halfway, so my sleep-deprived body stopped moving and awaited the warmth of his hug. We did not speak but quickly entered the car and took off. Soon we'd be able to discuss, but at that moment, we wanted to evacuate the presence of any authorities.

We were no longer in Youseff's Boca Raton confines but on Snoop's turf — Miami Gardens. The next several minutes Snoop navigated through back roads of a neighborhood with metal fences and large dogs monitoring the small homes. While Snoop focused on driving, I stayed focused on pulling out the merchandise from my bra's underwire. I removed the emeralds one-by-one and dropped each in the small velvet drawstring bag that Youseff held with his arms extending from the front seat. They made a clink as they met the others gems.

Soon we arrived at our destination, a gas station. The guys exited, and I followed their lead. Snoop approached a man with a smock sweating behind a metal drum and said *"Wah gwan!"* Introducing us to his friend, Snoop promised us the best chicken we'd ever had in our lives. While it was way past typical dinner time, there was a line wrapped around the pop up tent waiting for the delicious smelling food. I stayed quiet and reveled in the protective presence of Snoop and Youseff.

Youseff sensed a debate was taking place in my mind. *I had a good run. He'll understand that I'm done. He knows I'm not planning on doing this forever.* Since it was the first time that day I didn't have to wear a facade or suppress any indication of fear, I let my face relax.

He broke the silence and interrupted my battling thoughts, "I don't want that to happen again."

"Neither do I," I responded. "How'd you know I was being held?"

Youseff smiled. "Remember when I said that I always have an eye on you?"

"Yeah," I responded, unsure where his aimless question would lead.

My boss pointed to my neck. "That charm has a GPS tracker in it."

"No," I said, clutching the necklace. "You creep!" In any other situation, I would've felt violated that someone was keeping such close, unannounced watch on me. But today, Youseff had just saved me from being sentenced to years in a Colombian prison.

"When you're away, I make sure that you're on the route," he explained. "I saw that you were at the airport but then you left and didn't pick up my calls."

"And you pretended to call on behalf of the Ambassador?"

"The Ambassador," he chuckled. "Sounds so official! Armando and I are friends. I sold him his past three engagement rings." I should have figured; Youseff seemed to know everyone in powerful positions. He squinted his eyes. "But I don't know who tipped them off."

"A man was following me," I blurted.

"Soluna," he lifted his eyebrows. "Why the hell didn't you tell me?"

"I didn't want to concern you. I thought I might just have been paranoid."

"Your safety," he said, "is my biggest concern."

"I thought once I got to the airport I'd be safe."

"But you were in Colombia," he said, smiling. "The police are just as bad as street thugs." His occasional use of old-school vernacular confirmed he was older than I initially assumed.

"Promise me that if you ever feel like you are in the slightest bit of danger again, you'll tell me?"

"I promise."

My boss pulled me in for a long hug and pecked me on the top of my head, just like my dad had done after a nightmare or bruised knee.

"Thank you, Bling," I smirked.

"Oh no," he released his grip and let out an embarrassed chuckle. "What else did you learn?"

Before I had an opportunity to respond, Snoop returned with three styrofoam boxes overstuffed with jerk chicken, coleslaw, rice and beans. Hunched over, we settled on the curb of a parking spot and dove into our food without exchanging any words. Apparently, I wasn't the only one with a nervous stomach who hadn't eaten all day.

What would bring us — an older Jamaican man, a wealthy Jewish man and an unsuspicious blonde — together to share a midnight meal on a curb? The two million dollars' worth of diamonds and emeralds secured in the lockbox of the taxi.

28

Connor's face became dark red. "How could you be away from your phone for an entire twenty-four hours?" Veins on his forehead flared that I'd never seen before. "You're telling me you didn't check it once?" He wasn't stupid. He knew he was being lied to again. All of me wanted to come clean, but I couldn't. I'd made a promise to Youseff.

I didn't speak.

"I looked up your flight number and came to the gate to surprise you with flowers," he admitted. "Last night's dinner was going to be a celebration of our one-year anniversary."

A year? I ran into him on my first trip to Medellín which was in April...shit! He's right. It has been a year. I stared blankly back at him. "I'm so..."

He interrupted, "I looked like an idiot."

"I landed at Opa-Locka."

"That's what I saw," he said. He must have checked the official Passport Control system on my whereabouts.

"I caught a ride back in a jet with a friend of one of my investors."

"And that's the reason you missed dinner?"

The real reason I missed dinner is because I was handcuffed and detained in Medellín. I kept the truth in my head. "Yeah, but…"

"I don't know what else to do to get through to you," he said, clenching his fists. "You're so obsessed with this project, all the traveling, and your fancy investors. You're pushing away the people who love you…"

"That's not true," I protested.

"Your mom called me yesterday asking if you're alive, because you haven't returned her calls. She had no idea you were in Colombia." *Fuck! She did call me, last week when I was eating dinner at Youseff's house.* I inhaled.

"You blowing off dinner was the last strike. I'm done," he grabbed his blender which he'd use to make his daily morning smoothie and bolted towards the door. Without turning back, he yelled, "You need to figure your shit out!"

The door slammed, and the window shades shook. Lacking the energy to follow, I didn't chase him. The ignition roared and the gravel of the driveway stirred as his large pickup truck reversed. The vision of him standing at the gate waiting with a bouquet flashed. My body began to tremble, filling with guilt. I imagined him waiting for the final passenger to debark, just to be disappointed when he realized that I wasn't there. My secrecy was selfish, but vital.

A familiar cheery song shrilled from my purse. "Do you remember? The twenty first night of September..." The personalized ringtones was mom calling me again.

If I picked up, what would I say? "Hey, Mom! Sorry I couldn't chat this week. I was detained all day in Colombia. Connor just broke up with me. Oh and by the way I'm a criminal, but don't worry, it's all good. I made $40,000 in cash last night..."

The culmination of exhaustion and frustration erupted. I tried to push the tears back. Hearing my mom's favorite, upbeat song broke me. *Who am I turning into?*

29

The striking turquoise water glistened in the distance while soothing music hummed and incense danced throughout the meditation garden. Experiencing a lack of connectivity due to the cell-phone-free policy, I had no way to know if there had been a change of plan. Seth was an hour late for our meeting at the San Juan hotel's spa.

Did he get stopped at the airport? No…that's impossible! He's a veteran at this. He's probably just stuck in traffic. Everything is okay. I'm at a spa…relax!

As I was refilling my tea cup for the third time, the gates opened, allowing the Caribbean sea to reflect off his topaz-colored eyes. Dressed in a robe, he surveyed the patio. If being an actual physician didn't work out for him, he could always become a primetime television doctor with his dominating physique and exotic Middle Eastern-Dominican mix. I waved him down, and he approached.

"So why Puerto Rico?" I asked, trembling on my words. It had been months since I had seen Dr. Ramirez.

"I had a medical conference down the block. Really," he said while touching my arm. "Just an excuse to see you."

Is he flirting with me? My stomach swirled and eyes widened. "Well, I'm more than happy to have all our future meetings at spas," I joked.

"Don't get used to it," he said. "This was my cousin's way of getting you back in the game." Since Medellín, I'd taken time off to focus on the pharmacy partnership with Connect2Health. Youseff suggested a quick trip to San Juan, considering it was a domestic carry. Besides not having to pass through Customs, he was treating me to as many spa treatments as I could pack into a day. It had been more than a month since I'd seen the doctor in Santo Domingo, yet we resumed our banter like no time had passed.

"How's my guy Connor?" he asked, increasing the volume of his voice to compete with the bulldozing waves that met the rocky coast below. Each time that I saw Seth, he made a point to ask about Connor.

"He's good," I lied. "We're both very busy with work." I was still in denial about our fight, and not ready to admit that I hadn't spoken to him in two weeks.

"Tell him I say what's up," he said.

"Guess what?" I said, hoping to change the subject so he'd forget he ever asked about Connor. "Once we get the licensure, we'll start a pilot with three pharmacies in Little Havana. If all goes well in the next three months, we'll be in thirty of their other pharmacies around south Florida."

Connect2Health was about the only area of my life that I had a handle on and could provide answers for. I didn't want to feel vulnerable when I talked to Seth. He seemed to have everything in order: a tight knit extended family, a thriving medical practice, and a successful jewelry business. His high energy and capacity to get the most out of life challenged me.

I struggled to make direct, long-lasting eye contact. My thoughts fell victim to the quicksand of his gaze. The more I tried to resist, the more they pulled me in.

"I got you something," he said.

My head tilted.

"Our precious stones dealer introduced a new gem. It's called zultanite," he explained. "It's from northern Turkey."

"I've never heard of it."

"Neither had I," he responded and grabbed my hand tp slip the ostentatious ring on my finger.

"Since we are in the sunlight, it looks pink. At night, it turns amber," he continued. "And then under fluorescent light, it's green."

He beamed, excited to be teaching me something new. I held up the rectangular fuchsia stone and admired its contract against the sea. "Thank you so much. It's so unique."

He reached into his pocket and asked, "Sol, want a mint?"

I covered my mouth with both hands. "Does my breath smell?" I asked, mortified.

He playfully rolled his eyes and slid a box of mints in my direction. I picked up the unusually-heavy tin and placed it in my robe's pocket. He abruptly stood up and pecked my cheek, allowing the scruff of his overgrown beard to brush my face.

"I gotta run. My flight is in two hours," he said. "Hope to see you soon!"

I hoped so too.

30

The pickup was complete. The marathon of massages had my body feeling like a noodle so I posted by the pool in the afternoon sun. Laptop open, I was reviewing the final distribution contract for the pharmacies. Poolside chaise lounges had become where most of my work for Connect2Health was getting done - a welcome change from last year's corporate captivity.

"Ma, why you working?" A voice called from the pool. "You've got to enjoy your vacation!"

"I'm here for work," I said, hoping to avoid a conversation with a stranger.

"Well, you're fun" he sarcastically responded in a thick New York accent.

I looked up, pleasantly surprised at the appearance of my heckler. "Sorry that was rude," I replied. "I'm just trying to finish up my work before I order a margarita."

"Now that's more like it," said the man with the hazel-hued eyes. "Can I buy you that drink?" Initially, I baulked. Having been with Connor for the past year, I was accustomed to turning down any such invitations from random men. *He's cute. Hmm I don't have anything better to do today... Plus, I'm technically single.* That was the first time I'd found a positive of the breakup.

Leaving my laptop behind, I hopped in to join Nicky, the New York City native with amber eyes. He was in San Juan visiting his grandma. His cousin worked as a manager at the hotel, so he often spent time at the resort when in town. While wading with my shoulders hugging the edge of the pool, I frequently looked back and refocused my attention to the overheated tin baking on my towel. *Youseff's Rule #3: The product should never leave your sight.*

In the first few minutes of speaking with the man adorned with tattooed skin, I inferred he was the opposite of Connor. Nicky liked to take life as it came, while Connor always had a plan. Nicky condoned shady business, while Connor condemned it. Nicky made me feel dangerous, while Connor made me feel safe. Nicky was a vacation. Connor was a mundane weeknight.

The buzz hit. As I listened to him tell stories about how he was a professional boxer. I zoned out, entertained by my current situation. I was about to make fifty thousand dollars for enjoying the spa and then drinking by the pool. This is fun. *Connor would never drink with me during the day. He'd probably say it was childish.* Nicky touched my shoulder and gave me a suggestive look. We both were enjoying our spontaneous afternoon. *This is fun. Maybe it's best Connor and I broke up?*

As I took the final sip of my over-poured margarita, he asked if I wanted to join him at the beachside restaurant for dinner. I willingly agreed.

Our meal ended as soon as the bottle of wine disappeared; we relocated to the private, hotel-owned beach for salty kisses. To cope with the Caribbean heat, we entered the sea, allowing the powerful waves to crash against our naked bodies. A blinding spotlight turned on, and we squatted down. A man shouted from the beach. Nicky piped back in unrecognizable local slang.

With uncontrolled giggles, we gathered our sandy clothes, and our alcohol-induced escapade led to my presidential suite which boasted an aerial view of Condado's beach. We undressed again to reveal our sun-soaked bodies and slowly submerged ourselves into the hot tub on the balcony. He kept on his skin-tight athletic boxer briefs and thick gold chains. I watched the mint tin sitting on the nightstand.

Our flirty banter flowed, but I directed its course. I continued to ask questions about his life, in hope to avoid receiving any unanswerable ones about my own. I wasn't good at providing answers for my actual life. Lately, the unavoidable question — *What do you do?* — had become a crippling challenge. Explaining the contract with the Cubans or why I moved to Miami wasn't a simple one-liner. If I was acting as Myra, I was able to easily respond to these questions. The answers for Myra's alias were succinct and straightforward — everything my actual life was not.

During a lull in conversation, he snuck a quick kiss. He flirtatiously splashed water on my face and jumped out of the tub to go use the bathroom. A cascade of water flooded the deck. I observed how pruned my fingers had gotten, not realizing we had been in the water for so long. My eyes began to wander, awaiting his return. He'd carelessly left his phone on the edge of the tub which pulsed with vibrations from dozens of notifications. I had no intention of being nosy, but a specific message grabbed my attention.

¿Robaste a la gringa?

Like a switchblade, a sharp pain pierced my gut. The visceral reaction served as a karmic punishment for having let my guard down. I was about to get robbed. I needed to act quickly, before he returned; I jumped out of the hot tub. I opened his backpack and found a gun, knife, and duck tape. *Jesus Christ!*

The room began to spin. The abstract art on the walls swirled, and my heart thudded uncontrollably, matching the Latin trap music playing in the courtyard below.

I needed to buy time in order to escape. "Ehhhh....Nicky, don't come out here yet." I yelled. "I have a surprise." I took the weapons and secured them in the safe, plugging in the same four digit combination that I used for my gym locker.

"*Mama*, are you serious?" he chuckled.

"Just wait, please," I said and stumbled over my suitcase as my tequila-filled stomach gurgled. *Ugh! This is the worst time to be drunk.* I reached for my makeup bag and pulled out an unmarked tincture. I poured two shots from the minibar.

In order to escape my horny assailant, I needed to distracted him so I took off my bra and took a deep, long cleansing breath, pressing my arms against my trembling thighs.

"¡*Estoy lista!*" I called to tell him I was ready. He entered the room to find me topless, kneeling on the California King bed with my back curved and my chest perked, holding the contents from the minibar.

La Gringa

"Wow," he said in an overly expressive, complimentary manner. In that exact moment, he probably thought he was going to get the two things that he wanted that night.

"One more," I playfully suggested, and extended my arm with a shot glass.

"Ma, you're *loca*," he said, and made direct eye contact. "*¡Salud!*" We clinked glasses, and both of us slugged it back. He leaned in to kiss me. I turned away, allowing him to nibble my neck. To continue the illusion of foreplay, I offered to give him a back massage in response to him complaining about a recent intense workout. *No athlete would ever turn down a massage.* He lay face down on the bed and I straddled him, letting my hot-tub-soaked hair dribble on his bare back.

My hands sunk into his muscular back. I tracked his breathing, detecting if he was still conscious. *Come on. It shouldn't take this long to kick in.*

Within seconds, his body went limp. *It worked.*

While my date laid motionless on the bed, I began to frantically gather my clothes and stage the room. I transferred the jewels into the new sneakers which had a hollowed out soles for greater carrying potential.

His chiseled, golden body shook. His eyes opened and then rolled back, like something out of The Exorcist.

Oh my god! Oh my god! I snatched my phone and hit redial on the last number I called. *Pick up! Please pick up. It's only 1 am!*

Youseff answered after two rings. "Hello?"

I started to hyperventilate. "I think I killed someone."

"Soluna, calm down," he pleaded. "What happened?"

"I used the roofies. This guy was trying to rob me," I said, embarrassed of having gotten myself into the situation. "He's shaking. Oh my god..."

"Get a hold of yourself. It's rohypnol not cyanide," he calmingly stated. "He's fine! That means it's working. He won't remember anything after drinking it. But get out of wherever you are!"

"Fuck, fuck, fuck," I repeated, fluttering my hand that was free of the phone.

"The stuff lasts different lengths depending on the person," he said. "Soluna, who's the guy?"

"I'll tell you later. I gotta go." I hung up and attempted to steady my hand in order to write a legible message on the hotel-provided notepad.

Too bad you drank too much. We would've had fun in the hot tub. ;) - La Gringa

With Nicky incapacitated, I needed to unlock the weapons. I punched in the pass code to the safe. *3276...X! 3276...or is it 3275?* The tequila had officially kicked in, making the numbers of the keypad blurred.

After seven attempts, my jittery fingers finally entered the correct combination and unlocked the safe. I wiped off my fingerprints and returned the weapons to his backpack. Next, I emptied the contents of several more bottles down the sink. I sprinkled rum on the bed to make sure that Nicky awoke to the smell of a proper Caribbean hangover. I finished setting the scene by scattering the empty bottles on the floor and called the front desk to request a ride to the airport.

"Perdóname, señora. No entiendo," the woman said, unable to decipher my slurred words. I looked in the mirror to find my eyes dilated, skin flushed red, and mascara smudged. I closed my eyes, focusing all my attention on slowing my rambling. I caught my breath and repeated my request. She understood, and informed me that a car would be waiting for me in a few minutes.

Before exiting the room, I looked back at
Nicky. Drool dripped from his mouth. His eyes were
fixed wide open in the direction of the door. I shut
off the lights and attempted a brief prayer. *Hail Mary
full of grace the Lord is with thee. Your kingdom come that
will be....Ugh! What am I saying?* I hadn't recited a
formal prayer since I was forced to at my Catholic
high school. I had forgotten all the words.

Instead, I changed my approach. I abandoned
the prayer and was ready to bargain with the universe.
*If I get out of this, I'll never, ever, ever take Connor for
granted. I'll call my parents more. I'll donate twenty-five percent
of all the smuggling money. Okay, maybe ten percent. I'll go to
church...*

A burp erupted from Nicky's unconscious
body. There was no more time for empty promises to
my future self. I shut the door and fled.

31

The teeth markings on my styrofoam cup deepened as I nervously devoured its edge. The black coffee served as a necessary stimulant. The sun had not yet risen, and I sat in the airport's terminal awaiting the earliest flight home. I was furious with myself. There was nothing I could have done in Medellín to avoid the potential thief, but this entire situation was self-inflicted. *Did Nicky know I had the diamonds? Or was I just an easy target? How did I not suspect him sooner?*

I was staying in a penthouse suite that cost three thousand dollars per night. From that fact alone, Nicky probably inferred I was bound to have something worth taking.

The food court began to fill with budget airline passengers who were exhausted from their recent disagreements about unexpected baggage charges. The vocal travelers were ready to guzzle down greasy breakfasts to cure their all-inclusive resort hangovers. The subpar air condition in the terminal allowed the tequila to seep through my pores, reminding both my nose and brain of my bad decisions.

My eyes remained wide open the entire flight over the Caribbean Sea, ruminating over the fact there may or may not be a corpse back in my hotel room. *Will there be other suspects? Will the police think the weapons were mine? Will my trial be in Puerto Rico? Will I serve time in jail in Puerto Rico or Florida?*

The plane's cabin hummed as it brought me five hundred miles per hour away from the scene of the crime. The trip from the island dragged on as if it was a transatlantic flight. We passed over desolate, tiny islands. I wondered if they may be suitable places I could hide out if I was charged with murder.

After biting off all my fingernails, I occupied my hands by continuously readjusting my seat-belt, releasing and clicking it. I almost had forgotten I had one million dollar worth of diamonds with me. That was the least of my current concerns. Once the pilot announced our descent into Miami, I switched my phone on and incessantly refreshed my connection, hoping to encounter a sign of life.

During our evening together, Nicky checked on his latest notifications in the middle of the conversation. His insecure social media obsession had been one of the many behaviors that told me it was going to be a one night fling. Luckily, he was a slave to his virtual persona. I was confident that I'd find his profile.

Within minutes of searching posts tagged to the hotel, I found that *BronxBoxer92* had shared a photo of a lavish table setting from my hotel room's balcony. The asshole ordered breakfast and charged it to my account. His post was captioned "Mornings in San Juan." His followers who saw the post had no idea he'd woken up drugged, alone, and naked before snapping that photo. I exhaled in relief.

I prefer an expensive room service charge over a murder charge any day.

32

Since I didn't need to pass through Customs, I wouldn't see Connor. I'd have to ask him if I wanted to see him. I swallowed my pride and sent him a text.

Hey I am at the airport. Any chance you can take a break. Meet in the Admirals Lounge?

Once we deplaned, I retreated to the business lounge to recollect myself. A woman entered the bathroom and turned her nose up in disgust. I was scalding the back of my neck and using the hand dryer for my damp hair. I'd showered in the lounge in an attempt to rinse off the sweat and sin. I needed to destroy any evidence, so Connor didn't have another reason to question my erratic behavior.

The distance made me realize that he wasn't just my boyfriend, but he had become my best friend in this new chapter of my life. Even though he didn't know the full me, I couldn't go a day without a situation or joke that I wanted to share with him. The lack of communication led to self-conscious introspection, making me second-guess my past actions and words to him. In my professional life, there was a plan with systematic steps to reach a desired outcome. With Connor, there was no plan. Meeting him was not part of the plan.

He responded.

Be there in ten.

I nervously grasped the napkin dispenser on the table, giving my fidgety hands something to do. In the distance, I saw him check in with the front desk. Since he was dressed in his uniform, he was let in, no questions asked. Instead of just walking in, he stopped to sweet talk the old woman at the desk. He had a knack for making people around him feel good.

Watching him survey the lounge and then locate me, the last sentence he said to me at my home replayed in my mind: "You need to figure your shit out." Since then, he hadn't contacted me. But I hadn't reached out either. I wanted to give him space, but also not seem desperate.

I couldn't be truthful about the actual reasons for my unexplained behavior and this made me appear dishonest. I feared that he'd fallen for the illusion of me - confident, independent and driven. But once he'd got to know me, he'd seen the real me - opinionated, scattered, and over-committed.

La Gringa

My legs hugged the bar stool legs as I waited at a high-top table with several million dollars worth of illegally-smuggled gems on me.

He bowed his head. "Hi, Soluna."

He never calls me by my real name. Am I still in trouble? He settled into the seat across with a loaded pistol on his waist and the responsibility of combating undeclared goods from entering the United State of America.

The lack of sleep from the night before undeniably had an effect, but the lies and intricate cover stories were what drove me to exhaustion. I wanted more than anything to be entirely truthful about my overseas business and tell him everything: the reasons why I couldn't spend Tuesday nights at his house, why I missed our dinner plans, and why I really quit Shotzee's.

"Soluna, good to see you!" A familIar bartender at the business lounge asked, "Want the usual?"

"No, thanks." I said, ashamed that I had a *usual.* I knew the names of most of the bartenders and attendants, yet I only knew the names of two of my neighbors. Lately, I spent more time in this lounge than my own home.

La Gringa

Sitting in front of Connor, I felt more afraid and scared of the outcome of the impending conversation than when I was apprehended in Colombia. Losing him was losing the final tie I had to my old life. He was the only aspect of my current life that provided safety, stability, and a feeling of home.

"Where are you heading?" he asked.

"I'm actually on the way back," I responded. "Just a quick trip to San Juan."

"You're nuts!" He snuck a smile. I missed how amused he was by my comments. "The grocery store is a quick trip, not Puerto Rico," he said.

His playful injection of humor and the glimmer in his deep brown chocolate eyes, showed his willingness to compromise. Right then I knew our relationship was salvageable.

33

Growing up, we never prepared for storms up north. Instead, we reacted afterwards by shoveling snow which quickly turned to heaps of colorless sludge. The concept of precautionary measures before a storm was new to me. I began by bringing inside any item that could catch in the wind. As I dragged in the final potted plant, a small lizard scooted out and disappeared into my home. *Oh well...at least he'll be protected from the hurricane.* Next, I searched for anything of value and placed it on high book-shelves and the refrigerator. Storm surge was projected in my neighborhood, and my small house was in the flooding zone.

Snoop quickly beeped his horn twice, a courteous reminder I was late. The final stage in my hurricane prep was to wrack my brain for all the locations I had stashed money. Considering I was bound to lose electricity, there would be no alarm system; therefore my dad paranoid, yet realistic dad warned me that looting was a possibility.

La Gringa

Ah yes...the money in the vent. I almost had forgotten. I quickly grabbed a screwdriver and hopped on my couch to remove the metal air vent. I reached for the thick wad that was collecting lint and placed it in my suitcase.

Connor welcomed the opportunity to work. The hurricane didn't scare him. He'd earn double overtime and wouldn't have to be cooped up in close quarters with me who'd inevitably be on conference calls all day. In order to evade concerns from my parents, I told them that I would go to the Channel Ten studio with Caitlin. I figure that'd calm their concerns as they couldn't know where I'd actually be heading. From the excitement of Youseff, his Boca Raton bunker seemed to trump any of my other evacuation options.

I hesitantly entered the taxi, well aware that hoards of people were also vacating where the eye of the hurricane was destined to hit. Traffic was bound to be harrowing.

The media sensationalized the impending storm, encouraging everyone to properly prepare for the worst. Whoever came up with the saying "calm before the storm" never was on Interstate-95 gridlock between overflowing minivans of on the way to Orlando.

Two hours into our trip, we made it to the city limits, sandwiched in between backed up cars. Two men hopped out of the pickup truck in front of us and began to throw a football back and forth along the highway as their girlfriends stayed parked in the truck. Other passengers in neighboring vehicles followed suit, embracing an opportunity to stretch their legs.

We were stalled where the Turnpike and Interstate split and a noticeable building sat. Its long runs of neon announced its obstructive presence. The adult entertainment club in the industrial district was rumored to have been an old Walmart. No one knew too much about its past, but only what was currently housed under its roof — a basketball court, a barbershop, a large nightclub, many private rooms, a full restaurant, a photo studio and more. Regardless if you were driving northbound or southbound, each side of the building displayed a sign, 'King of Diamonds.' Like the eyes on the billboard in The Great Gatsby, the strip club's emblem greeted me each time I was on my way to or from the true *king of diamonds*.

34

The symbol on the corner of my laptop which represented the wifi's strength pulsed. I hoped the connection would stay strong. Youseff had promised it would. *It had to.* I needed to review feedback from patients and send out a proposal for Connect2Health's newest distribution partner, the largest health plan in south Florida.

The opera music blared from the massive speakers and consumed the hall where we sought refuge. We were cloistered in the lower level, Turkish-style area of his home that had no windows and thick cement walls. The spa was the safest area to barricade ourselves and wait out the storm. Youseff's family, some neighbors, housekeepers, Snoop, and I were camped out, surrounded by ornate tiled walls and hanging lanterns.

When the song concluded, I heard coos and calls from the east wing of the home. All the animals, originally housed on the grounds, were caged in the other end of the mansion, being watched by several well-compensated zookeepers.

Youseff's wife was brushing the hair of Lucia. On the lap of Lucia sat a very patient old dog. Like her mom, Lucia was combing the dog's whispy hair. Snoop sat hunched in the corner playing solitaire and sipping on a dark liquid. While I stayed hugged to my laptop, I occasionally looked up and caught Youseff smiling ear-to-ear for no apparent reason. I'd never seen the boss get tipsy before. He seemed to be enjoying the sips of Barolo and sounds of Andrea Boccelli. He walked over, stood in front of me and shook his head. I knew he was upset that I was working and not relaxing.

"Is Connor safe?" he asked.

"Yes," I responded.

"Is your home secured?" He swished his wine, inspecting its viscosity and not interested in my response. He already knew the answer.

"I think so."

"Then there's nothing left that you can do now," he said and clinked my glass. "Enjoy yourself!"

I closed my laptop and slid it in on the table. I stood up and joined in on the hurricane party. Lucia's full eyelashes batted at me, encouraging me to join her and her mother. Youseff's wife Solomiya was a picture perfect mom. She tended to her toddlers, attended fitness classes, orchestrated meals and kept active in her profession. A career I still didn't know the details of yet.

I grabbed my wine and scooted next to the makeshift beauty salon. I had met her countless times, but we never had spoken one-on-one. I figured tonight would be a good opportunity to change that.

"Solo, I can't believe I don't know this but," I continued. "How'd you and Youseff meet?"

She grinned. "About fifteen years ago," she chuckled. "Oh wow! I'm showing my age."

"Stop it!" I responded. With her porcelain skin and high cheekbones, she didn't look a day over thirty-years old.

"I used to travel as much as Youseff. While he was jetting down to Colombia, I took many trips to Poland."

"Yeah?"

"I worked for a Russian technology company," she winked, insinuating that it was her cover story. *Damn, even Solo is up to something?* "I'd fly to Krakow twice a month. One evening, my flight out was delayed. I decided to wait at an airport bar. You know how he is. He talks to everyone. So we started chatting and he ended up inviting me to join him for dinner at a seafood restaurant at the other end of the terminal.

"He tried so hard to impress me. He ordered a bottle of wine, oysters, steak and caviar..." She laughed. "Which was ironic..."

"Why?"

"Well, caviar was the reason I was going to Europe." She stated in a very matter of fact manner. I narrowed my focus, begging for an explanation. She continued, "A Russian man from North Miami Beach would pay for my travel. It was a great gig. I'd fly to Poland, be given a suitcase of roe, then have several days to take a train or hop on a quick flight to see my family."

In a few months, we'd no longer be able to have these types of conversations around Lucia. She was very smart for her age. She was already able to understand some English, Spanish, and Russian. Soon she would be catching on to the incriminating conversations the adults around her were having.

Solomiya elaborated. "Not just for free trips home, but it was decent cash to supplement my depressing salary from the deli." She was the only one from her family in Ukraine who received a visa to live in the United States. Her first couple years in America consisted of slicing cold cuts in the day and going to school at night.

"Anyways, we drank a whole bottle of wine. I don't even remember what we spoke about, but I remember we laughed non-stop. Our meal was interrupted by…"

Youseff butted into the story. "Last call for Solomiya Petrova!" He said mimicking the gate agent at Miami International Airport a decade ago.

Solomiya smiled. "I almost missed my flight, but I remember having such a good time with the stranger."

"It sounds like a movie," I said.

"Well," her face shrunk as she said. "Not really. So I was so rushed to make my flight we didn't have a chance to exchange numbers."

Youseff officially joined the conversation. "It was the biggest regret of my life. I was so mad at myself," he said, putting his arm on his wife's shoulder. "I tried to find her, but it was a different time than it is now. There was no social media. From then on, I'd head to the airport unnecessarily early in hopes of running into her again..."

"So how'd you guys reconnect?" I asked.

"A few months later, I was leaving Fontainebleau after a night of dancing. I had an early flight so I left the club before my girlfriends. At the taxi stand, a silly man in a hot pink shirt and flashy white pants jumped out of a taxi."

I smiled imagining the moment. She continued. "He refused to allow me to get into a taxi alone and insisted that Snoop drive me."

"God gave me a second chance," said Youseff. "I wasn't going to mess it up this time." He petted the dog on Lucia's lap and told Lucia how beautiful her almost-finished new hairstyle was.

"We stopped at my apartment to grab my suitcase and then went to the twenty-four hour diner near the airport before my flight."

"I made sure I got her number that night," Youseff winked.

The lanterns dimmed, and the music hushed. Youseff shot up. There were several seconds of uncertainty, a test to see if his recently purchased generator would put up a fight to Hurricane Irma.

Once the electricity proved it would be staying on, Youseff let out a victorious "Wahoo!" and fluttered off into the distance. He was transfixed in a giddy-like manner around ensuring everything was in order. He had laid out stations for all of his overnight guests. Each setup included a sleeping bag, flashlights, ear plugs, an eye mask, and face moisturizer. All of which were customized with our names.

"When I arrived home a week later, my apartment was filled with my favorite orchids. I guess

I had mentioned the exact species when we had our first meal at MIA. I don't remember, but still he's always been so thoughtful and conscientious in his gift giving," she said. "He's always listening..."

"For better or for worse," I joked. She laughed, wrapping a pink bow around Lucia's braid.

"Dating him was the most exciting time of my life. I never told him the reason of why I traveled overseas. He suspected something, but he never prodded. Just as I never did with his work. I was always discovering more about him. He revealed himself slowly. Not in a lying way, but in an elusive, intriguing sense." She gleamed. "Other guys I dated, I felt like I learned everything about them in the first date. But Youseff was different. I was always learning more."

"Caviar smuggling?" I asked. "Is that still a thing?" I couldn't wrap my head around that being a justifiable expense to travel all the way to Poland.

"The man I worked for ended up getting busted. Some of his friends contacted me to do similar jobs, but I didn't want to spend more time away from Youseff. Around that same time is when I realized I wanted to build a life with him. It wasn't worth the cash anymore."

I nodded my head. "That's a pretty awesome story. It sounds like it was all meant to be."

"I guess so! Fast forward, and here we are," she said and looked down at her slightly protruding stomach. The couple was expecting a brother for Lucia.

Throughout the rest of the evening, we savored and celebrated the reprieve from the demands of our day-to-day lives, all while Mother Nature was in full fury outside.

35

The hurricane hysteria dissipated as quick as it came. The hiatus made me realized I needed to tighten up some potential loose ends on my end. In my closet sat two shoeboxes stuffed full of hundred-dollar bills. With no security system and a curious boyfriend who spent every other night at my place, I knew this method of storing my hard-earned cash was irresponsible. Youseff suggested that I obtain several safe boxes and purchase strategic assets, like watches and jewelry, that would hold their value. To date, his recommendations had always been tactical and well-proven, so I decided to make monthly shopping trips part of my routine.

Snoop would drop me at Bal Harbour Shops: high society stomping grounds and luxury retail oasis, where the ratio of plastic to natural noses was disproportionate. Like navigating a Latin American airport, I was there on a mission. In an afternoon shopping spree, I'd spend the same amount of money that I earned as my salary from last year.

The familiar yellow vehicle approached, and I heard Snoop shout, "Baby, that you?"

I laughed at my reflection in the taxi's windows and looked around, hoping my neighbors wouldn't see me. I dramatically cleared my throat and mimicked the accent of my European cousins. "*Alo*! My name is Tasha. I dance," I said, pointing to the logo of *E11EVEN*, a twenty-four-seven strip club, on my trucker hat. "We go to the mall to spend money from..." I stuttered, "*loooo-creeetive vikend.*"

I entered the car to continued howls of laughter from the front seat. Snoop was amused at my discomfort with the sleazy image I was portraying. This was my go-to disguise when I went to launder my earnings. "Baby," he said, "if you really want to commit to this new look, you need some surgery."

I readjusted the two-sizes-too-big push-up bra under my snug neon tank top. My voice resumed its usual tone, "Thankfully, I'm not that committed."

"You're a crazy white girl," Snoop snickered. "You know that?"

He wasn't wrong. I looked ridiculous. "Thanks, Snoop. It means a lot coming from you," I sneered.

"The boss called," said Snoop. "Are you in for a quick Mexico City trip tomorrow?"

As of that morning, we'd received approval from the State of Florida for Connect2Health, but now we were waiting for the Cubans to set up the technology at the Havana office. No work could be done until I got the go ahead from Guido.

Hmm... I've never been to Mexico. Besides, I might as well make the money... "Sure, why not?"

We inched through the gridlocked afternoon traffic. Snoop and I bobbed to the reggae music and I watched the day-to-day lives of people play out at each backed up intersection.

My eyes met with a woman around my age sitting at a bus stop. She wore a business suit and blazer in the sticky Florida humidity. She held a folder tightly and fanned her face with it. She was checking the times posted on the bus schedule. By the size of her conservative heels, I assumed she was heading to a law or accounting firm interview. Our eyes locked. Without exchanging words, I gave her an encouraging nod, hoping my comforting look could help calm her apparent nerves.

"Snoop?"

"Yeah, *mama*," he responded, and looked up in the rearview mirror to meet my eyes.

"I want to buy you something as a thank you gift for always being there," I said. "But I've no idea what to get you."

"Baby, as long as the sun is shining and I have my health, I don't need anything." Even having left Jamaica, he kept a jovial, care-free outlook on life — a foil to the chaotic, anger-inducing rush hour traffic that he battled every day.

"Can I ask you a question?" I said. "You tell me if it's too intrusive."

"Shoot!"

"Are you paid per hour or is it a retainer situation?"

"I'm not sure what all that means," he chuckled. "But money appears in my account every other week."

"How'd you meet Youseff?"

"The universe wanted us to meet," he responded.

Snoop told me how he'd immigrated to Miami in 2006 and took the first job available: driving a taxi. During that same year, Youseff made over forty round trips to Colombia via Miami International Airport. Within a stretch of two weeks, Youseff jumped into Snoop's cab three times while departing the airport. The men believed two times was a coincidence, but three was fate. On their third encounter, Youseff offered Snoop eight hundred dollars in cash if he were to be his personal driver for the rest of the week. Ten years later, he was still driving for Youseff.

"He paid for all my mom's medical bills when she got sick," Snoop said. "He even skipped an overseas business trip to organize a funeral for her that we would have never been able to afford."

"Have you ever thought of working somewhere else?"

"Never," he said. "He even paid for my daughter's nursing school and helped get her a job at Mount Sinai. Do you know any job that has benefits that good?"

"You have a daughter?" I asked, shocked that she'd never had come up in our conversations.

"Two," he responded and reached for his wallet to show me photos of smiling faces that I'd never seen before. "I'm forever grateful for what he has done for me and my family. Behind all the flash, he's a good man."

I pressed the fake eyelashes to my eyelids to ensure they were fixed to my face.

36

I juggled the phone between my ear and shoulder as I hurtled through the terminal. Even though it was a terrible, inopportune time, I needed to take the call. I hadn't spoken to either of my parents in a week or so.

My dad's deep voice sounded excited. "Soluna, sweetie! You'll never believe it!"

"Hey Tata! What's up?"

"I don't remember when, but I guess I entered myself in some Harley-Davidson contest," he said.

Yes! It worked!

"I totally forgot about it," he continued. "Well, guess what?"

"What?"

"I woke up to a delivery of a new bike in my driveway."

"Get out! That's wild!" I said. "You need to send me a photo."

"This bike is awesome! It's the exact model and color I wanted."

Earlier in the week, I'd negotiated the purchase and delivery of a custom motorcycle to my dad's home, ensuring a counterfeit Harley-Davidson letter was delivered with it. Both my parents thought I was barely making ends meet by working at Shotzee's and living off my savings from my several years of corporate servitude. They had no idea their daughter had enough money to fund an enviable savings account for a person on the brink of retirement. Just as they never expected the source of my actual income, they were oblivious to the fact that recent and upcoming surprises were bankrolled by my criminal activity.

"Tata, I'm sorry, but I'm about to board a flight. Can I call you later?"

"Where's Carmen Sandiego off to now?" Like pop music in the Balkans, his pop culture references were also a decade behind.

"Mexico City."

"Mexico?"

"Since the licensure approval is taking forever," I stalled. "Catherine and another investor want me to talk with some people in Mexico to explore if the Miami Project's model could work there." It wasn't entirely false. Youseff was in fact a pseudo-investor, and the Mexican-American population would be the next natural progression of the business. While I couldn't lie to my dad, I couldn't tell him the truth.

"I can't keep up with you. Fly safe! Talk to you later."

"Love you, Tata."

Recently, if there was an issue or challenge in my life, I'd throw money at it. A solution would present itself. But in working with the Cubans, money didn't matter. I had to wait. As hard as I pushed, there was no equivalent to Coppelia. There was no one-dollar fast lane with The Miami Project or doing business with the Cubans. Just like the bankrolled international companies who hoped to work with the government of the backwards island, I needed to wait in the same line. Money could not buy time. I simply had to wait for my ice cream. As a disillusioned American, I assumed I had a privilege that I could skip the line or buy time with money. But in Cuba the expression "buy time" doesn't translate. Time could not be bought and money had no effect on speeding things up.

If I was doomed to this waiting game, I decided I might as well stockpile as much money as possible so I had money when it could actually help push the business along. Feeling assured that my dad's surprise had gone according to plan, I now needed to devise a way to deliver my mom her surprise: $45,000, the amount of money needed to franchise a mobile dog-grooming business. Since her retirement from the airline and my relocation to Miami, she'd moved to Sarasota to live with Jerry, her Budweiser-drinking ex-pilot boyfriend. Maybe because he was the polar opposite of my dad or I hadn't given up hope on my delusional Parent Trap-inspired childhood dreams of my parents being together, but I'd never connected with Jerry. He made my mom happy, so I had no rational reason to disapprove.

Since I'd inherited my mom's need to be in constant motion, I knew an idle retirement wouldn't suit her well. She'd often tossed out the idea of owning a mobile dog-grooming business. I thought eliminating the barrier of money would be a tipping factor for her to pursue her second career. I needed to be more creative in getting her the money than I had been with my father.

"Last call for Mexico City!"

I arrived at the gate disheveled and breathing heavily. I pulled up the boarding pass on my phone and waved it in front of the reader. Once it beeped, I charged ahead down the boarding ramp. Luckily, I had a three hour flight to strategize how to inconspicuously get my mom her gift.

37

*Welcome home! Change of plans. Meet Snoop at
Latin America Café. He'll bring you to the party since we need
it ASAP. DO NOT talk to anyone. Go upstairs, turn right,
and go to the 4th door on the right. See you soon & plz hurry!*

While simultaneously reading the message
from Youseff and checking my email for the licensure
approval, I placed my passport under the Global
Entry kiosk scanner. The process of entering the
country while catching up on my other, more
honorable double life had become second nature. The
thrill was gone. I no longer felt the adrenaline
pumping through my veins like I did during my first
few trips. When I began taking these assignments, I'd
enter back onto American soil with a million dollars
in gems and a huge sense of accomplishment.
Recently, traveling for Youseff felt like a rush-hour
commuter adhering to a mundane timetable. The
excitement and novelty of international air travel had
vanished a longtime ago.

"Ma'am, please come this way!" said an
unfamiliar, commanding voice. I abandoned the

monitor's prompts and turned around to find Connor's supervisor. Without saying a word I tilted my head, questioning with my eyes if I were in actual trouble.

"I'll have to send you to Agent Lopez's line," said the teddy-bear-shaped man, whose shirt was uncomfortably tucked in to his protruding stomach.

"Thank you, sir!" I said, and approached the desk.

"Good evening, miss," said Connor. "Why'd you leave the country?" He took my passport and placed in on the scanner.

"I had to get away from my boyfriend," I joked.

"Yeah, I don't blame you," he responded. "The dude sucks."

I grinned and said "Come on! He's not that bad." I nervously readjusted my bra, because a jewel was violently poking into my rib cage.

Connor smiled and stamped my passport. "Welcome back to the United States of America, Miss Hill."

"Good to be back."

As I turned to walk away, he blurted, "Sol, can I spend the night? My A/C is still busted."

"Yeah, of course! But I won't be home until way later. I'm going out with Jared for Art Basel." That week in Miami was an annual festival in which the jet-setting glitterati gathered for a week of excess, opulence, and overpriced art.

"Have fun with all the artsy fartsy people. They've been coming through all day. Quite an interesting bunch..."

"See you at home, officer," I said, and darted away with several million worth of diamonds on my person and in my luggage. Earlier in the week, I'd relocated the majority of my cash and newly-purchased luxury goods to a safe box at a Coral Gables bank. I still had random, relatively smaller piles of money hidden throughout my home in unassuming locations, like the five thousand dollars in the ice cream box in my freezer; Connor was lactose intolerant.

I figured several thousand would be easier to explain than the eight hundred thousand dollars that I had accumulated to date.

38

The drop off location was on Star Island, an island of top-shelf real estate that sat on a bay which served as a moat to its inhabitants' off-limits lifestyle. Despite the countless times I'd dashed by on my way to Miami Beach, I'd never been set foot on it. Snoop rolled down his window to greet the guardsman.

The guard readjusted his belt and lowered his head to the taxi. He locked eyes with Snoop. "You must be lost, boy."

Snoop stayed quiet and looked in the rear view mirror. I opened my door and got out. "Excuse me," I asserted. "My family is hosting the party on the island tonight." I handed the Israeli ID to the guard, and he retreated to his post.

"*Bumboclaat,*" Snoop mumbled under his breath. Having been with Snoop in other situations where he was disrespected, I'd begun to pick up other Patois swear words.

The guard returned shortly and said, "Welcome back, Myra! I have you in the system from this morning. Next time please let us know your name, and I'll look you up."

I snatched it back. "If you ever ask my driver if he's lost again, your job will be the only thing that is lost," I got back into the car and let out a dramatic exhale. Snoop accelerated onto the magical, forbidden land.

With my skin color, doors were opened. With his skin color, questions were asked. It was unfair. Nothing I could say could properly communicate my sympathy or ease his seething frustration and hurt. Instead, I introduced a question to change the subject. "Snoop, so Myra is in town?"

"Baby, I don't know. I only know what I need to know." His ability to go from being disrespected to sweet and loving was admirable, almost saint like.

We pulled up to a mansion with light beams projecting into the moonlit sky. The front lawn hosted a Lamborghini, an armored Range Rover, and a chrome-wrapped Bentley convertible. Snoop's car was worth as much as a single hubcap on most of these vehicles. I never understood how these so-called "philanthropists" could drive a car that costs the same as feeding an entire impoverished village for a year. *But then again, who am I to judge?* Recently, every time I'd tried to pass moral judgement on someone's decisions, I'd wound up retracting it after gathering additional context. I'd come to realize that there was always more to the story than one could initially infer. My newly-learned behavior of withholding judgement may have been the only objectively positive character change that I'd undergone since moving to Miami.

The massive front doors of the waterfront home were propped open by a disheveled man orchestrating the steady stream of caterers. The staff members, all dressed in black, brought in platters of bite-sized food for the highly-anticipated vegetarian molecular gastronomic experience. Considering the event was a fundraiser for Youseff's animal-rescue charity, all the food was meatless; an example of the thoughtful yet extravagant intention that went into every detail of his party.

As I reached the top of the staircase in the foyer, I heard a distinct, recognizable cackle. I froze and looked out the window to see Keekee in the courtyard. *What the hell is she doing here?* She often did random one-off bartending or entertainment gigs. *Why is she dressed like a geisha?* I stayed hunched over and crawled the entire length of the hallway so she wouldn't see me. She'd blow my cover and recognize me even in my disguise. She wouldn't be able to take a hint if it hit her in the face.

The fourth door on the right opened to an expansive bathroom with tropical wallpaper and golden-framed antique photos of jaguars. I sat at the vanity to remove the contact lenses; I'd finally gotten the hang of using them, and they no longer irritated my eyes. For the first few months, it looked like I had chronic seasonal allergies.

I began to take out the gems from under my shirt and place them into a long, slender plastic medication organizer that I'd snagged from a partner pharmacy of Connect2Health.

The door creaked open, and a woman entered. "I hope you aren't getting me into too much trouble," she stated.

I looked in the mirror at my humidity-curled hair and then at her straight dark brown hair. The real Myra and I looked nothing alike. At that moment, I understood why Youseff recommended I dressed a certain way the past year. Not because he wanted me to blend in, but to mirror the understated confidence and poise that Myra wore.

"Great to meet you..." I stood up and turned towards my alter ego. "In real life!" We hugged like relatives who hadn't reunited in years. "I've heard so much about you." Besides sharing a passport, we shared an unspoken, instantaneous bond from our gem-smuggling sisterhood: similar experiences, international contacts, and fears.

"Same with you!" she said. "Both Youseff and Seth speak very highly of you." She turned to ensure the door was shut, and no one would hear what she was about to say. "Don't tell Seth, but I never hear about Cristina. He's always talking about you and that business of yours." Cristina was Seth's fitness-model fiancé that he mentioned when I first met him in Punta Cana. Since then, I'd never heard any more about her, even after asking about her. Instead of an update, he'd respond with a change in subject.

"He's awesome," I said. That was the only comment I could say without making it obvious that I had a schoolgirl crush on her cousin.

"Are you staying for the party?"

"I wasn't planning on it. Are you?"

"No. I'm not much of a partier," she shrugged. "Plus, I have the red-eye to Israel."

"What brought you to town?" I asked, while admiring the carpal-tunnel-inducing diamond on her finger.

"To see a friend's gallery opening, and for what you brought me."

I snatched the pill sorter off the counter and handed it to her. She opened it to reveal the meticulously-sorted jewels and laughed. "Youseff always has the most creative containers."

"I actually came up with that one," I pridefully replied.

"You really are as good as they say." She nodded her head. "Here, this is for you," she said, handing me a large envelope. "Bling said he put another five in there as a make good for being late on last week's payment."

The heavy envelope held several bundles of hundred-dollar bills wrapped in rubber bands.

"There should be a hundred in total," she stated.

"This is insane," I said, peeping into the envelope. "He's going to need to start wiring me money."

"Yeah, I don't recommend ever having this much cash on you. Please be safe!" she said and placed her hand on my shoulder. "Soluna..."

"Yeah?"

"Please stay for the party. It'd make the guys' night."

She exited and closed the door behind her. I sat in the dark bathroom with a decision. I needed to change and dump the cash, and I had two options. I could keep the envelope at my house, while running the risk of my overnight guest finding it. Or I could store the money in a locker at the gym. Either option I chose, I planned to bring the money to my deposit box first thing in the morning. If I went to the gym, I could stop at the nearby department store; I didn't have anything in my closet trendy enough for Art Basel's most prestigious party.

The standstill, tortuous traffic was the tipping factor in my decision. The journey to my home and back would an hour more than the drop off at the gym. The electricity of the party was undeniably magnetic. I needed to return as soon as possible.

An hour later, I returned in an outfit that cost me two thousand dollars, an amount worth more than my current wardrobe. I justified the expense by telling myself this night was the first time I was celebrating anything since moving to Miami. I'd always wondered what it felt like to take advantage of the nightlife that the city was well-known for, so I selected a boisterous metallic dress and funky, colorful shoes on a mannequin at the department store. I didn't even look at the price tag; I just paid with twenty hundred dollar bills. I faked an accent, making up a story that I was in town for an exclusive yacht party, and the airline had lost my luggage. The aliases, with all their back stories and foreign accents, were coming way too easily.

39

"Miss, would you like a photo?" a man asked.

"Of course," I responded. "It's not everyday you get to snuggle a sloth." The camera flashed. I held the delicate jungle creature close to my chest.

The moment guests arrived at the party, they were greeted with an opportunity to be photographed with an animal. All in hopes that their snapshot would grace the high-society section of the Ocean Drive magazine's next issue.

Someone called from the distance, "Soluna!" When spoken by him, these three syllables had the power to send my stomach on a skydive. I readjusted my grip of the sloth and slowly turned towards Seth. Apparently, he had taken advantage of being in the Miami sun, darkening his olive skin.

He disengaged the conversation he was in and walked towards me. I returned the animal to its handler and anxiously swayed side-to-side in anticipation of his arrival.

"You look beautiful," he said, reaching for my hand. He twirled me around, showing off my glittery dress. "I can say that now, since you're not dressed as my cousin. Right?" He winked.

I kissed him on the cheek and whispered in his ear. "It's always nice to have my investors in town." If I were to attend the party as Soluna, it was planned that I was there under the premise that Seth was an angel investor in Connect2Health.

He continued to hold my hand as he led our way to the backyard. Amongst the party was an outdoor gallery of high-end jewelry pieces. A plexiglass dance floor was secured over the pool and several monstrous yachts served as the dramatic backdrop.

We approached a group congregated in front of an oversized ice statue shaped as a peacock. Seth began to introduce me to his childhood friends, all of which had archaic, biblical names that I didn't know people in this century still used: Shlomo, Ishmael, and Chaim. Most of these people I knew from detailed stories I'd heard from Seth over our meetings in Santo Domingo, but in keeping with my current, truthful persona, I pretended it was my first time hearing anything about them.

Before finishing my first glass of wine, I was introduced to a seemly-endless line of celebrities.

La Gringa

From Miami's mayor to the Dolphins' quarterback to a world-renowned Brazilian street artist, anyone who was anyone in Miami was at this party.

With an inviting aura and a snake-skin silk shirt, my boss approached the circle and asked, "Can I get anyone a drink?" I reminded myself that this version of me had never met him before.

"I'd love a glass of red," I responded.

"Malbec?" Youseff asked.

"How'd you know?" I nervously smiled. He turned to direct a server hovering behind him to fetch my drink.

Seth said "Youseff, meet Soluna. She founded that company that I invested in. The one that does work with Cuba."

"Great to meet you, Soluna. Welcome," he kissed my cheek and pointed to my shoes. "I love your Lou's!"

"My what?"

"Your shoes!"

My head tilted, but I accepted the compliment. "Thanks." Next week over dinner in Boca Raton, Youseff would educate me about

Christian Louboutin's influence on the luxury shoe industry.

Seth interjected to cut the awkwardness. "Youseff is my cousin, and also the host of this ridiculous party."

"Well, thank you for having me!" I looked around. "It's incredible."

"Ridiculous?" asked Youseff. He shot a darting look at his cousin and raised his arms showing off the swirling stimuli behind him. "It's a celebration of art."

"Didn't the *Herald* describe the party 'as if Willy Wonka filmed a rap music video at a synagogue'?"

"That's correct," Youseff said dismissively. He turned to me. "I'd like to learn more about this business of yours." The bystanders nodded in agreement. "Who knows? I may want to invest."

"We connect Spanish-speaking patients in America to video appointments with doctors from Cuba." I explained. "You may have seen that pharmacies are now offering the ability to talk to a doctor on demand. We're the service behind it."

Youseff asked, "So how much money are you looking to raise?"

"We aren't taking on any more investors at the moment," I said. The truth for why I didn't need investment was that Youseff and all the gems in the jewelry surrounding us were bankrolling the entire business' operations. While I kept the truth in my head, Youseff kept his focus on me. "We want to prove the concept locally before we take on more money."

"That's not very Miami of you," Youseff said. The group laughed because most inhabitants of the city were more than comfortable spending other people's money without a guarantee they'd be able to pay it back.

"But, don't worry! We will be expanding soon," I added. "Let's stay in touch."

"I'd like that," he said. He removed a thick card from a gold container and handed it to me. His acting was so convincing that for a moment I thought he'd actually like to become an investor. Then I remembered what he'd reminded me a few weeks ago. 'Soluna, we can never be on the books together in business. Our family is under close watch' *I still need to ask what they were under watch for.*

Our group's conversation soon transitioned to the evening's main attraction: The Evil Eye Auction. Every year, a jewel-studded pendant in the shape of an eye would be auctioned and all of the proceeds would go to Youseff's animal-rescue charity. This piece of custom jewelry became a cherished status symbol for south Florida's philanthropic community, as men would purchase it for the special woman in their lives. Last year, the coveted necklace sold for nearly a half a million dollars. According to Jared, Jay Z had been bidding on it for Beyoncé, but he got caught up smoking a cigar on the terrace with Youseff and missed the final round of bidding. Stories spread about the party, which ultimately drove up the value of the pieces sold at the event. Youseff's Art Basel party had become as infamous as Diddy's White Party.

All previous winners would wear their evil eyes to the event. The elite couples whose long-lasting love was embodied by the piece worn around the women's necks sat at a designated VIP section guarded by a muscular black man, a gigantic Russian and an intimidating Latino body builder. The larger-than-life security detail communicated through earpieces, monitoring all potential threats to protect the tens of millions of dollars seated at the table.

While Youseff hosted the iconic party to raise money for his charity, most didn't realize that the evening also helped him liquidate his excess inventory for the upcoming holiday season. The dude was a genius - an absolute mastermind. While he did truly help people with his charity events, he was always personally financially benefiting behind the scenes.

Amid the crowd, I saw a face I knew. Caitlin, my friend from the gym, was holding the arm of a guy that looked like he'd stepped out of an Abercrombie catalogue. *Damn, she has a type!* She dated men who looked like they were the captain on the lacrosse team at an Ivy League school. They all wore a constant smirk on their face because they enjoyed the comfort of a healthy trust fund. I introduced Caitlin to Seth and spoke with her for a few moments. I didn't make too much of an effort to engage with Brock. They didn't seem to be hitting it off. I doubted I'd ever see him again.

Keekee joined our table still in uniform, dressed in a skimpy silk kimono on a break from her body sushi assignment. She took out her makeup compact to pat down her foundation and use the mirror to scan the party's guests. "Gurl, there are so many daddies here!" Keekee said, announcing her excitement to the entire group. She loved older men, and older men loved her youthful, free-spirited energy. She'd go daddy hunting by positioning herself around Miami at cigar stores, expensive golf courses, and any establishment that would be patronized by men who had high-school-aged children.

She added a much-appreciated, unfiltered infusion to the conversation. While everyone's attention laid on Brock who was telling a boring story, Keekee looked Seth up and down and smacked my thigh under the table. With complete disregard for who heard her, she said raising her eyebrows, "Um, total *papi!*"

I gave her a side eye and said under my breath, "Don't even think about it."

For a fleeting moment, Keekee, Caitlin, Brock, Seth, Youseff, and Jared sat together. I remained silent and scanned the table, realizing that every person knew a different side of me. Jared knew me as the waitress that didn't take shit from rude guests. Seth knew me as the healthcare startup founder grappling with the uncertainty. Youseff knew me as the blonde with a knack for evading suspicion at foreign borders. Keekee and Caitlin knew me as a spin class record holder. *God knows what Brock thinks of me?* Based off his first impression, he may have thought I was a well-dressed party girl who had wealthy, influential friends. His perception was the least accurate.

Seth was zoning out from Brock's anti-climatic story and staring at my hand, specifically the finger which wore the zultanite ring that he had given me in San Juan. The jewel sparkled and changed its color each time the strobe light hit it. My eyes met his gaze, and I smiled.

Just like the zultanite, everyone at this table knew me in a different light. But like the ring, Seth knew the most of the muddled mosaic of who I was — one gem with multiple colors depending on its environment.

Keekee's fifteen-minute break was over, so she retreated to her post. Youseff and Jared used the interruption in conversation to excuse themselves to check in on the party.

Brock shared that his family owned the building which served as the Magic City's lava lamp. Most Miamians didn't know the name of the colorful building, but everyone recognized it as it captivated everyone's attention regardless of your vantage point. The tall, prominent structure apparently changed color by the press of a button on Brock's phone. He could alter its hue and speed. Previously, I'd assumed the colors that danced on the skyscraper were random, but like all things amongst Miami's elite, there was more than met the eye.

Brock turned to me and asked, "What's your favorite color?"

"Green. Like an emerald green," I said, hoping that Seth across the table heard my response. We locked eyes, exchanging more than any words that could fill the time.

Brook exclaimed, "Look!" He pointed to the building across the bay. The skyscraper was now illuminated in the deep green color as requested. The party's high-society guests held the keys, or in this case the buttons, to the city.

Brock and Seth stayed engaged in an intense conversation over LeBron's departure from the Heat — a topic I had no input or desire to be included in. Caitlin and I relocated to the dance floor. We started to move, ignoring the other party goers and fully feeling the effects of the free flow of wine. I looked back at the table. Seth was amused by our tipsy dance moves and shot me a supportive smile.

Out of the blue, Caitlin turned to me. "Do you know what Ross is up to now...business wise?"

"Come on girl, we're partying," I responded. "I don't want to talk about that creep."

"You're right," she said apologetically. "Sorry that I asked."

The salsa music came to an abrupt stop, and confetti guns exploded over the dancing crowd. A conversation-stopping lion's roar rumbled through the speakers to quiet the guests, and Youseff waltzed on stage holding a lemur. I let out an explosive laugh. The man was constantly outdoing himself. *He's so over the top!*

La Gringa

Our host welcomed the crowd and thanked guests for their generous donations. Like an Olympic medal ceremony, he invited the winning bidder and his wife to the stage and dramatically clasped the Evil Eye on her. The necklace was the statement piece of all statement pieces. It outdid any designer or luxury jewelry product because of its exclusivity. Only one was created per year. The emeralds which glimmered on stage were the same gems that had been strapped to me in the holding cell in Medellín. Hundreds watched the gracious recipient radiate with joy as Youseff secured half a million dollars' worth of jewelry around her neck.

Next, Youseff introduced to the crowd the night's main entertainment, Dr. Dre-idel. LED lights pulsed, and smoke machines let free. Jared started his deejay set with dramatic jungle noises mixed over deep house music. Once the beat dropped, waitresses dressed as aliens emerged from the back of the stage to hand out glow-in-the-dark shots brimmed with pop rocks candy. Dancers on stage began erratically draping the trees with Jared's product, the sparkly toilet paper. *Where am I?*

After spinning levers and pressing buttons, Jared flicked up his large headphones and looked up to see the party goers enjoying the music. He spotted me and snatched the microphone to announce over the futuristic beats, "Shout out to my favorite *gringa* in the house!"

I grabbed Seth's shoulders, attempting to dodge the laser beam that Jared began to shine on me in the center of the crowded dance floor.

40

The clunking sound of an erupting espresso pot woke me. A Category 5 hangover was about to hit.

"Good morning, party girl," said Connor. The smell of eggs and bacon filled my home.

"What time is it?" I groaned, lifting the covers over my face to dodge the midmorning sun barging through the window.

"It doesn't matter," he said. "I'm leaving now. Go back to sleep."

"Connor?" I called. I tried to remember how I had gotten home, but everything after Jared took the stage was fuzzy.

"Yes, babe," he patiently responded while grabbing his keys.

"I met a sloth named Bernice," I said then hiccuped. "Oh, and there were aliens and a chocolate fountain."

"Someone's still feeling it," he laughed. "Good night! I left some water and Advil next to the bed."

"Thanks! Love you," I called out.

Wait...I've never said that to him before. He knows I don't mean that...right?

I pulled the comforter over my face and slept for another hour. The last time I had drank that much alcohol was during my Smirnoff-soaked teenage summers. The only way to rid myself of the horrid hangover was to sweat out the diabolical toxins that I had subjected my body to the night before. After mustering the energy, I left my home to wallow in the sauna and scoop my bag to drop its contents at my highly-secured deposit box.

I entered the gym hiding behind sunglasses and a hood. I pitied whoever had to look at my sunken eyes and puffy face. Once I turned the corner to the locker room, my stomach dropped. Thick yellow tape covered the entrance. *DANGER / PELIGRO*. The lockers were all swung open, revealing their emptiness. My breath ceased, and I grabbed the arm of a protein-filled personal trainer passing by. "What's going on?" I asked.

"Didn't you read the signs?" he questioned. "There are locker room renovations all week." Without acknowledging his response, I charged to the lobby; I needed to find where they were storing the items that had been left behind. The unenthusiastic front desk attendant led me to a utility closet that housed forgotten water bottles and yoga mats. My recently-purchased hot pink bag was nowhere to be found.

My body tensed. I realized someone discovered the cash. *Fuck!*

The security footage must have caught me hauling the bag; now I was bound to be part of a money laundering investigation. *Why was I so lazy to leave the money at the gym? Why'd I pick such a eye-catching colored bag?* This whole situation was sloppy and rushed. I was angry with myself because my desire to return to the party and see Seth clouded my decision making. I was smarter than this. *Youseff's Rule #4: A job is not done until it is done.*

The impatient gym employee lurked behind me in the doorway as I rummaged through the pile of miscellaneous items. After a long minute, she let out an aggressive sigh and said, "Clearly, it's not here. Would you like to leave a description of it? We'll keep an eye out for it."

What was I going to write? Pink duffle bag with a casual hundred thousand dollars inside?

In that moment of despair, I realized that losing a hundred thousand dollars was better than being subpoenaed on suspicion of money laundering. I took a deep breath to collect myself. I turned around. "Thanks for your help, but there's still a chance I left it at my friend's house." I forced a smile.

While confused, she was unbothered by my response as this meant she could return to her hunched-over position watching videos on her phone. Defeated, I exited the utility closet.

A door to the spin studio opened and a soft voice called out, "*Chama, ¡ven aqui!*". María, a cleaning woman, motioned for me to meet her in the vacant room. Once she closed the door and ensured there was no one else in the dark room, her concerned face turned to a mischievous, loving smile.

"*¡Tranquila! Tu bolso está en mi casa.*" I exhaled and wrapped my arms around her fragile frame. My heart which was on a high speed car chase had come to a screeching halt. She went on to tell me that she'd snatched the bag earlier in the morning, and it was currently being guarded by her husband at their home. Since most other people on the cleaning staff had sticky hands, she knew the money wouldn't last more than a couple hours in the Lost and Found.

"*Mami*, I know you work hard. I don't know what you do, but I like you," she said. "You look at me in my eyes, and you ask me how I am doing.

When I am in this," she said, pointing to her scrub-like uniform, "most people here act like I don't exist."

María was a high-school teacher in Venezuela, but forced to flee because of her husband's rare health condition. She explained that one day they went to the pharmacy and his medication was gone, with no understanding of when it might be available. For them, coming to America had been a matter of life or death. She never complained but was always smiling and thankful. She gave me her address and encouraged me to hurry, since her *marido* would soon be leaving for his afternoon shift.

Within ten minutes, I arrived at the complex which sat a few lots back from *Calle Ocho*. Leaning on its recent paint job, the building looked as old as the city itself. It tried not to show its true age, like most people in Miami.

The front lawn was overrun with malnourished chickens and an enterprising *abuela* hustled tropical fruit to the cars stopped in traffic. While opening the gate, I heard a man yelling from the second floor window, *"Gringa, espera!"*

I appreciated how Latinos were very matter-of-fact with nicknames based on one's physical appearance. María's husband had never met me before, but he was confident I'd respond to the name.

La Gringa

There were countless *Flacos, Negritos, Rubias* and *Gorditos* throughout Miami.

The stout, friendly-faced man met me on the porch and led me to their quaint, second floor studio. We stayed quiet. He understood no words would calm my nerves until I laid my eyes on the cash. He swung open the pantry door to reveal the duffle bag. I lunged forward, unzipped it and let out a long, shuddering breath. The terrifying thought of money laundering charges vanished.

"*Muchas gracias*," I thanked him, offering him a tight hug. *How can I properly repay him and María?*

He patted me on the back. "Now that you have your *dinero*, let me make you a *cafecito*." He invited me to stick around, either because he knew that I needed some caffeine to cut through the visibly apparent hangover, or he figured he'd learn where all the money came from.

He began the conversation explaining that he understood the terrible feeling of something wrongfully snatched. It was like the hurt he felt for the political hijacking of his beloved Venezuela.

During us chatting, I took out a healthy stack of hundred-dollar bills and placed it on their table next to a ceramic figurine of Virgin Mary and several framed photos of their distant relatives. From my recent practice of holding money, the amount felt like ten thousand dollars.

At first, he refused the money. I tried several several attempts of proposing different ideas of how they could use the money. Once I explained that María wouldn't have to work additional night shifts, he agreed to keep it.

"*¡Eres un angel,*" he said. His comment was sweet, but the truth was simple. If I was caught, the authorities would consider me a criminal, not an angel.

41

Our northbound trip, a routine drop off, veered towards the center of the city — an area left out from the development dollars. Snoop parked on a street lined with jewelry repair stores and makeshift cardboard beds for the roaming beggars. The street was a jarring juxtaposition of haves and have nots — Hublots and homeless.

"Where are we?" I questioned.

"Downtown."

"No shit," I snarked. "But, like, what's that?" I pointed to an old building where there was a busy stream of people entering and exiting.

"The Seybold building," he answered. "It's a landmark."

It stood tall compared to the other buildings on the block, but its height didn't compare to the gigantic, modern financial building hub nearby across the river. Next to its entrance, a semicircle of men congregated sipping coffees at a *ventanita*.

"Call the boss," Snoop said. I let out a sigh, asserting my annoyance for the unannounced detour. While waiting for Youssef to pick up, I watched Snoop pull from the glove compartment a dozen or so IDs and flip through them like paint samples. *What's he doing?* I took a deep breath. *Ugh Youseff, pick up! This is annoying!*

I recently hired my first full-time employees for Connect2Health. I told them I would be at the office before the end of the day. I wasn't appreciative of Youseff's surprise stop because I intended to keep all the promises I made to my newly formed team.

Youseff answered. "Hello, *mi gringa!*"

"What's going on?" I badgered.

"I need you to do a quick pick up," he stated.

"Why didn't Snoop do it earlier?" My flight was delayed so I knew he'd been killing time while waiting for my arrival.

"Come on," he replied. "You know that wouldn't work." He was right. The men in bullet proof jackets guarding the entrance would question Snoop, while I could slip through unnoticed. At that moment, I realized what Snoop was doing in the driver's seat.

"Okay," I paused, knowing there was no way out of this. "Which identity should I use?"

"Does Snoop still have Kim?" Youseff questioned.

I put the phone down from my ear and asked. "Snoop, do you have Kim?" After several seconds of fumbling, he handed me a Massachusetts driver's license.

"I got it," I said. The voice on the phone began to laugh.

"What's so funny?" His carefree demeanor contrasted my impatience.

"The Kimberley Process."

"The what?"

"The Kimberley Process," he explained. "It's the international trade agreement aimed to combat the trade of blood diamonds."

"The more you know..." Truthfully, I didn't want to know. The less I knew the better. I didn't want to be aware of the domestic or international laws that I broke on a weekly basis.

Kim Peterson was a 32-year-old, blue-eyed 5' 4" organ donor from Massachusetts who left her driver's license at a South Beach nightclub. The innocent-looking blonde was probably unfamiliar of her name's significance in the diamond industry and certainly unaware of the crimes that her identity was committing that afternoon.

"Sol, wear sunglasses. Their cameras use facial recognition," he continued. "Oh and don't look at what he gives you."

"Got it," I responded. Instead of contesting or questioning, I wanted to get the errand done as soon as possible so I could make it to the office by the end of business day. "You owe me." I said and hung up.

I approached the entrance and passed two large men loading a Brinks truck. As they hoisted stuffed bags, the muscles overflowing from their bullet proof vests flared. Up until recently, I didn't realize how paper bills of money get heavy. Last week, I helped Youseff move duffle bags of money from his garage to the safe in his office. My arms were sore the next day.

The Seybold Building's ground floor boasted dozens of shops reselling Rolexes and diamonds set in countless variations. Diamonds brought all type of people together: the seasoned, meticulous craftsmen, the nervous men ready to propose, and the ballers drowning their insecurities in carats. Despite the surrounding sparkling stimuli, I made my way to the corridor where two men in suits with top hats and curls stood next to food delivery men waiting for the elevator.

My imagination kept me entertained the entire climb to the tenth floor. I wondered what was really in those food delivery bags. I questioned any type of package I saw people transporting. *Were there really empanadas and croquetas in there? Or just stacks of straight cash?*

I located Suite 1090 and pressed the doorbell. It buzzed, and I pushed open the windowless door.

An unusually hairy man draped in gold stood behind the counter.

"I'm here for Youseff," I stated.

He smiled and said, "I know."

"How?"

"People like you don't come to this floor," he chuckled and disappeared to the back room.

My eyes inspected the walls covered in faded photographs of customized jewelry - bedazzled Jesus pieces, gold-plated names, and over-the-top diamond-studded jewelry.

He returned and extended his arms to hand me a paper bag.

"How long have you been working for Bling?" he asked.

I grabbed it and my hands dropped before I recognized its actual weight. "A year or so," I responded.

What is this? It's too heavy to be diamonds and way to heavy to be cash? Is it gold?

"Why have I never seen you?"

I crumpled the bag to compact its size and immediately regretted not bringing a purse.

He continued to press. "Damn, I would have asked you to dinner already," he said.

The man continued to speak, but I left without a goodbye and before the creepy propositions continued.

What am I carrying? He'd never know if I peeked. I descended to the lobby.

I didn't want to look because I feared to know what I was transferring. But I did want to look to discover what else Youseff was up to.

I reentered the lobby. My nail sliced open the tape of paper bag. My curiosity trounced by my obedience.

It can't be that bad. He wouldn't have me carrying it if it was that bad. Right?

My eyes locked with a familiar face.

"*Mama*, what are you doing here?" Not only did Rafa have questions for me when stamping my passport, but it appeared he had some this afternoon as well.

"What are YOU doing here?" I stuttered, turning the question on him so I could use the time to figure out what I was going to tell him why I was there.

He stuttered. "I was copping a Cuban link for myself."

"Let's see it," I asked.

"Okay, *mama*," he said and looking around. "I'm actually here because I'm buying a shorty some ice." There was no reason he needed to tell me, but recently, I discovered the more I let people talk, the more they let out incriminating information.

I pursed my lips, pretending to be shocked. He didn't need to tell me he was buying jewelry for another woman for me to know that he had other girlfriends in addition to his fiancé.

"Well I won't say anything if you don't say anything," I bargained. I looked down to confirm my phone was off because I didn't want anyone to over hear the impending lie. "I'm here because I'm buying Connor a chain."

"Oh *mami!* He's going to look fresh!"

I grinned because Rafa bought the bogus alibi, but also picturing Connor wearing a gaudy chain. *He'd never.*

"Please don't tell him you saw me. Promise?" Rafa had the memory of a goldfish, so I wasn't too concerned he'd tell Connor about our run in.

"Pinky promise *mama*," he said.

"*¡Adios!*"

A bout of guilt manifested itself the same way as a punch to the gut. Running into Rafa was instant karma for going against Youseff's orders. I reset the tape and closed the paper bag.

I never saw what I was carrying, and Rafa never mentioned the run in to Connor.

42

Youseff shared with me the security code to one of his several garages. I barged in unannounced. I assumed he'd be in his study because he spent the hour before dinner checking in with his lieutenants across Latin America. The mornings were reserved for conspiring with his European and Middle Eastern contacts.

He must have seen me on his security camera footage because he awaited my arrival, wearing a mischievous smile. "Hello, Ms. Thirty Under Thirty!"

I rolled my eyes. "It was nice of her to nominate me," I said and settled into the chair facing his desk. "But Connect2Health patients watch Telemundo, they don't read Forbes." Caitlin used all the pull she could with her friends in the media for opportunities to promote my company. She insisted. I never asked.

"Enjoy the limelight lady," he said. A few years ago, I would've dreamed of such an accolade, but now such awards seemed to be an immature, pathetic way for people to masturbate their professional egos.

I reached for the small package in my suitcase and placed it on Youseff's desk. He didn't open it but continued inspecting the large diamonds.

"Myra will be in Panama next week," he stated, readjusting his spectacles and keeping his attention on the glimmering object in front of his face. "How does a quick in and out trip sound? I need to replenish our supply of yellow diamonds."

"Which day?" I asked and opened my calendar.

"Thursday."

"As long as I'm back by Friday morning," I responded. "I have an important meeting."

"Perfect!" He set down the seven carat flawless diamond and jotted something on his notepad. He looked up. "Sol, do you like ham?"

"Do I like ham?" I repeated. "Uh yeah, why?" He pointed to the corner of the room where the floor-to-ceiling bookshelves met. There sat a large leg of *Iberico* ham wrapped in a red bow.

"Some Spanish guy that we do business with sent it as a gift," he laughed. "It's all yours!"

"Why don't you want it?" I asked.

"It's not kosher."

That night, I left his home with a twenty pound piece of meat in one arm and a hundred thousand dollars in the other.

43

"*Pasajeros, el vuelo a Miami está demorado treinta minutos,*" the man on the loudspeaker repeated. "Passengers, the flight to Miami is delayed for another thirty minutes." Thunder shook the lounge in the Panama City airport. Exhausted travelers were stretched out on rows of seats or any horizontal surface they could claim. Disinterested in the soccer game blaring from the television, I burrowed into a couch near the window, hoping the heavy downpour of rain would drown out the rowdy sports fans at the bar.

If the flight boarded in thirty minutes, I'd still have enough time to do the drop off in Boca Raton and make it back to Miami for the nine o'clock meeting with the reporter. If the flight was delayed any longer, I'd have to reschedule the interview. I began to draft my apology email.

Hi John, I'm so sorry, but I am unable to make it this morning. My flight returning to Miami was delayed last night...

La Gringa

I hoped I wouldn't have to press send in a few hours. In order to stay awake for the next announcement, I scrolled through my social media news feed, filled with photos of life milestones and insecure public oversharing. I felt worlds away from my childhood friends, geographically and metaphorically. Our priorities were so different and became more polarized recently. Every other photo album was a pack of girls in horrid matching t-shirts with Nashville or Las Vegas as the backdrop. *Who'd make their best friends do this? Who as an adult would willingly wear these?*

I sent Youseff a message.

I have an idea...

44

"You're out of your mind," Youseff laughed. We sat on the lower-level terrace which overlooked large, colorful plastic containers. He'd recently rescued a family of sea turtles who were recovering in pools speckled throughout his backyard.

"Come on. Just think," I explained. "A group of tipsy bachelorettes rolling through Customs. No one would expect it."

"You're not wrong," he said before taking a puff of his cigar. "But Soluna, what are we talking about? Ten million dollars worth of inventory?"

"Give or take," I wobbled my head. This amount of inventory would get Youseff and the entire jewelry business through the end of the year.

"You want to use your friends as mules?" he asked.

"Not USE them," I said, searching for the correct verb to clarify. "But GIFT them. I'd be treating them to a nice stay. Plus, what if I was able to guarantee that Connor would be working that day?"

"That'd be nice," he said shaking his head, "but it is too risky."

"I know almost every agent. We'd only get caught if the girls knew what was going on," I explained. "You know I won't tell them anything."

"It's too risky, Soluna."

"Hear me out." I stood up. "A childhood friend of mine is currently planning her bachelorette weekend. We're deciding the location in our group message now," I said, holding up my phone. "What if I say I have a villa we can stay in Punta Cana and all they need to do is pay for their flight?"

He leaned back and closed his eyes. His fingers rubbed his temple. Deep in thought, he spoke. "Are they all *gringa*?"

"Yes! All Irish Catholic."

He sunk his face into his palm. "Which weekend do you need the villa?"

The weekly trips to Latin America were taking a toll not only on my relationships, but now they were affecting the business. Connect2Health was taking off. With last minute meetings and troubleshooting the technology, my presence in Miami became more and more essential for its sustained expansion. The idea that I proposed to Youseff would allow me to transport the amount of gems in one trip what would take me an entire two months if I were to do it on my own. Not only would he not have to pay for all of my travel expenses, but this idea would enable him to have ten times worth of his precious inventory in one day.

Youseff understood that this may be his only option, but he needed to discuss it with his cousin. While he desperately needed more merchandise, my boss respected the agreement that he made with me from the start. He vowed to never allow my smuggling career to get in the way of actual career.

Two weeks after my proposal and presumably many discussions between the cousins, I received a message on my outdated, flip phone.

Seth looks forward to hosting you ladies next month.

45

The weekend was intended to be filled with classy dinners and relaxing beachside massages, but the intoxicating tropical environment had different plans. The bachelorettes couldn't resist the fully-stocked bar, compliments of Seth, so the trip turned into drunken debauchery on par with Girls Gone Wild. The celebration ended Sunday morning with self-loathing and regret, which was temporarily put on hold once the alcohol began flowing again. The girls weren't ready to face their impending reality and were making Bloody Marys for breakfast.

I hadn't eaten a proper meal my entire time in Punta Cana. I avoided drawing any concern by moving food around my plate. While food was unappetizing, the rum went down easily.

I couldn't relate or muster up the care to participate in the conversation. While they were discussing options of colors for the bridesmaids' dresses and the names of babies of high school classmates, I was focused on the rollout and execution of Connect2Health's biggest deal that following week.

I had nothing to add to the conversations. I remained quieter than usual, fixed to my laptop in the kitchen and stuck in my own head.

It was the last morning of our stay at the villa. Four days had passed, and I had yet to hear anything from Seth or Youseff. We never discussed the specifics of how exactly the carry would occur. The last I'd heard from Seth was the evening before I'd left Miami. He'd sent a message.

Everything is handled. Enjoy your vacation and the time with your friends. See you at the villa!

I kept scrubbing the marble kitchen countertop surrounded by the girls who were picking at the fruit plate. Despite the home having a full-time housekeeping staff, I found solace in keeping my hands busy by assisting in household chores. *If only I could find such an activity for my brain.*

I had wondered if everything was actually handled. *Does Connor know I'm planning this? Maybe he reads the messages from Youseff when I'm sleeping and he's been waiting for a big carry to bust me. A sting like this would for sure get him the promotion he wanted.*

The doorbell rang. I saw Seth's black Maserati parked in the far end of the driveway. The housekeeper opened the door and he entered, holding two magnum bottles of Dom Perignon and an overflowing bag of obnoxious party favors.

"*¡Mis amores!*" he said, greeting the girls. I kissed him on the cheek and turned to introduce him.

"Ladies, this is the infamous Seth," I announced. "You can thank him for the bottomless booze this weekend." I began to point. "Seth, this is Emily, Kara, Christy, Kelly…"

Seth interrupted. "I'm sorry, but we need name tags. I don't think I'll be able to remember all your names."

The girls stood silent and dumbstruck, staring at Seth as he hijacked the conversation. Fiona, the most boisterous of the girls, attempted to match his energy and began to ask him questions about his life on the island. He enjoyed her banter and flirted back.

"Sol, I see all you Missouri girls have some attitude," he joked.

While Seth's gaze appeared to be focused on topping off the bubbly with a spritz of orange juice, Fiona made a wide-eyed darting look, trying to get my attention. "What the fuck…" she mouthed, fanning herself. "He's so hot!"

Seth noticed from his peripheral vision and asked, "Would you like me to turn up the air conditioning?"

"No, no! I'm fine!" she said, turning bright red.

Once all the flutes were filled, he led a toast wishing the bachelorette happiness in her marriage. He then presented the group with bachelorette-themed costume-jewelry necklaces.

"Please go enjoy the sunshine," he encouraged. "I saw that it was fifteen degrees in St. Louis today."

The girls scurried to the patio to savor the warmth. I stayed back, wiping the countertop and cleaning the same surface again.

"What are you doing?" he asked while grabbing the rag from my hand. "You're on vacation!"

"Vacation?" I chuckled. "Right!" I placed one of the gaudy necklaces around my neck.

"See these green beads," he said, pulling me closer like we were preparing to tango.

"Yeah," I responded nervously.

"When you land, you're going to take them. Those beads are the diamonds and these here are the emeralds."

"You've got to be kidding me," I said. I raised the necklace to my eyes to inspect the craftsmanship. Next, I held one diamond bead in my palm. It felt to be about the same weight as a penny. "Twelve carats?" I questioned.

"Actually thirteen. But close," he nodded his head, impressed. "The emeralds are fifteen. There are five emeralds and five diamonds on each chain."

"You're insane."

"Let me remind you," he said. "This was all your idea."

I took a gulp from a glass that one of the girls had left behind.

"Eh! No booze for you," he demanded, grabbing it out of my hand. "You need to stay sober. You're about to have the carry of your life."

"Shhh!" I begged, and raised my hand to his mouth.

He winked his thick dark eyelashes. High-pitched laughter shrieked from outside. We turned our attention to the patio where my friends had started to feel the effects of the mimosas. They were taking photos of their topless backs overlooking the edge of the infinity pool.

"This is my cue to go," he said. Seth made sure no one was watching, then grabbed my head with both hands. He looked me directly in the eyes and and kissed me on the forehead. "Make us proud, kid."

That was the first time he kissed me in a way other than the way you would kiss your great aunt.

Well, the first time that I remember. The photos I found the morning after the blurry Art Basel party flashed in my mind. They captured us very close in the backseat on the ride home. I deleted them immediately, concerned that Connor would get the wrong impression if he ever saw them. *I'm certain...well almost certain that nothing more occurred between the doctor and I.*

The limo arrived. My heart quickened its pace. I turned the music down and rallied the girls. *It's game time!*

46

The entire ride to the airport, I was attacked with questions from my friends. "How have you not gotten with him?" "Is he really a doctor?" "How do you work with him when he looks like that?" "Does he have brothers?" They didn't let up.

I managed the questions but remained focused. As we piled out of the limo, several girls tripped from losing their balance. We were a scene - ten loud, buzzed American girls in a foreign airport. *Everything is going according to plan.* Since I was the only one who spoke Spanish, I became the Mother Goose guiding my drunken ducklings.

Passing through security was easier than I'd imagined. The Dominican airport employees were thoroughly entertained by the drunk, giggling *gringas*. While holding rifles, they made flirty comments most of which my friends did not understand.

Before I knew it, we were headed down the boarding ramp. My incessant travel had its perks. I was given a seat in the front row of the plane — a perfect vantage point to see my unknowing mules all at once.

As I was buckling my seat belt, a man approached and said, "I love your group's necklaces. Can I have one?"

Jared wore oversized headphones around his neck and a goofy smile. *Youseff would send him. What's he going to do to help?*

"Sorry, you had to be at the bachelorette party," I said. I avoided eye contact with him since I knew he'd make me laugh. I couldn't acknowledge that I knew him.

"Bummer!" He said. "Well, excuse me, miss. I have the window seat." I stood up and let Jared into the row.

As my friends passed through the aisle, he leaned over me and struck up conversations with all the girls who weren't wearing an engagement ring. He ended up purchasing and sending a bottle of champagne back to them. He treated being on an airplane, the same as if he were at a nightclub. As unpredictable as Jared was, his presence was comforting and added to my confidence. He was the closest thing to Seth or Youseff without having them actually on the flight themselves.

La Gringa

We didn't speak the entire flight, but exchanged side-eyed looks and corner of the eye smirks.

47

When we disembarked at the Miami airport, the babysitting began. We made multiple stops to the bathroom before we arrived at the line for Customs.

Everyone besides me was tipsy. *It's perfect.* This was the plan - to have all the girls be so distracting that no one noticed we walked into the country with ten million dollars worth of jewels draped around our necks in plain sight.

Despite the terminal being ice cold from the pumping First-World air-condition, sweat dripped down my brow. I wadded my forehead. While we twisted through the roped-off line, the foreigners stared at our group as if we were zoo animals. Americans were accustomed to over the top bachelorette parties and what they entailed, but the out-of-towners were entertained by the matching t-shirts and oversized necklaces. *Are they staring because we look ridiculous or they notice our incriminating accessories? Are we that obvious?*

I attempted to evade the darting looks by standing on my tippy toes to see if I could spot Connor at the desks. I checked my phone for a text back from him. *Nothing.*

Why isn't he at a desk? He isn't trapping me, is he? If he was arresting me, he'd have popped out already, right?

The girls kept chatting, but I didn't speak. I continued to manically thump my passport against my thigh. The line was maddeningly slow. I gazed across the large hall and was envious of international business travelers who were buzzing through the fast lane to get on with their day. Since most of my friends only left the country once or twice before this weekend, their pristine passports and lifestyles didn't require Global Entry. As much as I wanted to take advantage of the fast line, I needed to stay with my merchandise.

Next, I looked down and admired the zultanite ring's rare shade. The airport was one of the few places that the ring showed its lime green side due to the oppressive fluorescent lights. The millions of dollars worth of emeralds draped around our necks did not change a shade. I refused to believe Seth, the cousin of always-thinking Youseff, would give me a gift that didn't have an ulterior purpose. *Does the ring have some hidden purpose like the GPS necklace? Could it be bugged?* I twirled it around inspecting it for a miniature microphone.

The girls stayed consumed in trivial, to-fill-the-time conversation. I entertained myself with a game I'd often play by myself while crossing borders. I wouldn't look at which passports the travelers were holding but analyze every aspect about their person and belongings. I'd look at the shape of their teeth. *Braces or no?* I'd gaze at the brands of their sneakers. *Adidas or Nike?* And then based off several conscious and many more unconscious biases, I'd guess their nationality. Next, I'd look at the cover of the passport. After much practice in this game, I was able to guess roughly nine out of ten travelers' nationalities.

While I passed the time in the line, the girls kept disrupting my focus and asking me about Connor. As much as the girls wanted to see him, I did not want to. When I was carrying the jewels and saw him, I felt guilty. I wanted to get to Boca Raton as soon as possible and finish the job. I didn't want to situations for the next few months.

Five girls were at the desks speaking to agents. I smiled making eye contact with an agent who was monitoring the crowd. He saw my confident smile, but did't hear the thud of my heart or see the the puddle of nervous sweat on my back.

I stood next in line for the desk manned by an older agent. I didn't recognize him. He wore thick glasses that I was confident he couldn't decipher the difference between the plastic and genuine gems draped around me. The person in front of me took back her passport and left.

I walked up to the desk. "I didn't call you," said the grumpy agent.

My eyebrows raised, taken aback by his rudeness. The man punched a few final things on the computer and then fled the post. I looked around to see if I should jump to a different queue.

"Look who's back," a spirited voice called.

"Hey Rafa!" I called as I approached the desk. He settled into the desk to begin his shift.

"*Mami*, Connor showed me those tight photos from that mansion," he said loudly. "My girl is right. She says you white girls are so over the top with bachelorette parties."

I laughed and nodded my head. *She's not wrong.* "Where's Connor?"

"He's in the back, some sketchy bro from Russia brought this bootleg computer." In classic Rafa professionalism, he revealed details that probably should've never left the interrogation office.

"Got it," I smiled and looked around, trying not to ask more so I could get out of there with as little conversation as possible.

"You joining us for happy hour tomorrow?" he questioned.

"I don't want to look at alcohol after this weekend, but yeah. I'll be there."

"*¡Bienvenida!*" he stamped my passport.

Their hangover hit midday as the girls waited for the connecting flight. In order to retrieve the gems, I informed my friends that I was waiting around with them until Connor's shift ended so I could ride home with him. Actually, I was sticking around to finish the job. When they were enjoying their mimosa-induced afternoon *siestas*, I discreetly snatched the diamonds off each strand. I made it look like I was fidgeting with the necklaces, but when no one was looking, I'd place them in my pockets.

After an hour of careful plucking, I still needed to secure the diamonds off of two more of the girls' necklaces that they kept around their necks. The flight was about to begin boarding. *Fuck! I need those necklaces.*

"Ladies," I stuttered. "So I have another bachelorette party next weekend. Mind if I take these?" It was a flagrant lie, but the girls didn't question it. They didn't even ask whose party I'd be attending because they were so preoccupied with the anxieties of their responsibilities that lay ahead that week that they willingly handed over their necklaces. *That was easy. Damn! Why didn't I do this an hour ago?*

I accompanied my oblivious transporters to their gate for their flight where they would be thrust back into the land of black ice, puffy coats, and winter weight gain.

The friend who was due to be married pulled me aside. "Sol, you're the best! The villa was a dream come true. Thank you so much!"

I looked down at the necklace that she proudly wore which was missing several beads. I gave her a tight hug and said, "No really, thank you!"

48

Tiki torches burned and flamenco guitar played. The seafood spread had enough food to feed the entire gated community. I descended down the stairs slowly to the candle-lit table in the courtyard and arrived to a slow clap from a dozen or so seated guests. I took a dramatic bow, as if I had just stuck a 10/10 landing in a gymnastics routine. That night we were celebrating the most valuable carry in Levenfiche Jeweler's history.

The group had not begun to eat, as they were awaiting my arrival. Connor thought I was out on Miami Beach with Keekee and Caitlin. "Dinner and drinks with the girls from the gym" had become my most common alibi for dinners in Boca Raton.

I was granted the seat of honor — the head of the table opposite of Youseff. My boss stood up to lead a toast.

"Cheers to our imaginative, daring," Youseff paused, "successful *gringa!*"

La Gringa

Youseff's wife, his older brother, a partner of the jewelry business, the groundskeeper, several animal trainers, Snoop, the family's rabbi, a few more people I had yet to meet and I toasted our goblets of wine. All of us were normal-looking members of society, but all accomplices in our boss' ornate international schemes.

The warm humid evening air matched the feeling that consumed my body; accomplishment and a freeing sense of relief. Surrounded by the nearest thing I'd ever had to a close extended family, even an ordinary weekday dinner felt like a special occasion. The palms swooshed, and the smell of citronella lingered.

Crazy ideas no longer seemed so crazy. From ideation to execution, my bachelorette party smuggling idea had come to fruition in less than two months. I stared up to the glowing window of the den where I was first introduced to my boss. I was promised cash, but received so much more.

49

"Dame una colada, por favor," I asked the woman behind the window. The sticky afternoon air called for Miami's legal cocaine alternative. I adventured down the block to fetch the much-needed stimulant, *café cubano.*

I'd begun spending almost every afternoon at pharmacies to oversee the in-store video consultations. Listening in on as many of the interactions between patients and the doctors served as the best way for me to improve and ensure the service was running smoothly. Previously, I had concerns that there may be a tension between the Cuban doctors and the American patients, many of who defected from Cuba, but on each call I oversaw, there remained an inexplicable, unspoken bond and understanding. Something that could not be clinically quantified. I was relieved to learn it wouldn't be a roadblock in Connect2Health's expansion.

While I waited, a news announcement grabbed my attention. I redirected my gaze to a small television behind the counter. On the screen, Caitlin stood in a jewel-toned dress in front of the condominium complex from the night I tried to forget.

Shit! I forgot to call her back! Caitlin had called me three times that morning. When I was onsite at a pharmacy, I had tunnel vision. If Connor, Youseff, my parents or even Catherine called, they went straight to voicemail.

I tuned out the loud, clanking espresso machine to listen. "Breaking news! Ross Perkins, Founder and CEO of HealthVentures, was arrested earlier this afternoon for the largest-ever Medicare fraud in the history of Miami-Dade County. "

Footage played of uniformed men escorting Ross, handcuffed in pajama pants and a bathrobe, to an unmarked car. The newscast returned to Caitlin, and she introduced the lead investigator of the case.

The stern, seasoned FBI agent waited for her to finish. "Ms. Mahoney, I know this is not what we spoke about before the cameras started rolling, but I have something to say before we discuss the details of the case."

Caitlin's eyes widened, concerned that the conversation would be going off script.

"Your investigative journalism provided our task force incredible intel in making a case against Mr.

Perkins," he continued. "Channel Ten should be proud to have such a diligent, inquisitive reporter. Thank you, Ms. Mahoney."

The broadcast continued as the federal agent elaborated on the meaning of Medicare fraud and the illegitimate business model that Ross and his colleagues had created.

My stomach sank. *Thank God I didn't get wrapped up in that bullshit! Did the firm know about plans for this sketchy business model? Did Jon know? Or was Ross playing all of us?*

Caitlin thanked the agent and turned to the camera. "Medicare fraud isn't just about money. The crime affects innocent patients and inhibits progress for the dedicated people who work hard every day to improve America's broken healthcare system. Back to you, Jorge."

The camera didn't cut out immediately but stayed on Caitlin enough time to show her uncontrolled smirk transition to a victorious, glowing smile.

My heart filled with warmth. She did this for me. Not only was it her well-thought-out, strategic way of helping her friend, but she'd done it in a way that would ensure more jail time and public attention than a sexual assault case ever would. By knowing her poise and patience, she was probably plotting retribution on Ross ever since the day she found me crying in the locker room.

"*Tu café*, lady." The woman inched the *vasito* closer to me. I didn't blink. Tears fell from my face: tears of sweet revenge, tears of joy, tears of relief, and tears of love. That was one of the kindest things someone had ever done for me. She never once told me her plan, but she saw it through until completion.

Despite trying my hardest to avoid any sight of his name, I'd unintentionally came across a news article last month that explained Ross received forty million dollars in his divorce settlement. *Why is he never happy with what he has?* He pushed a little, just to lose it all.

An impending conversation had been dancing in my subconscious for some time. After seeing Ross in handcuffs and a jolt of *café cubano*, it became clear. I needed to speak with Youseff. My luck would only last so long. Connect2Health was serving over a hundred patients a day, and seeing thankful patients was more rewarding than any multi-million dollar smuggling job that I had completed.

The woman handed me a napkin. I wiped the mascara trailing down my cheeks.

50

"Here you are," I said, handing the taxi driver with a loose hundred-dollar bill that I found crumpled in my purse. I didn't want to disturb Snoop by asking him for a ride. He seemed to always be on call. I wanted to respect his Sunday evening, especially because he'd recently become a first time grandfather, and was taking his responsibilities very seriously.

I was dropped off at a coffee shop in a strip mall a half mile from Youseff's neighborhood. Since visitors needed to be on a particular list, I changed into my Myra disguise and put on athletic clothing. I pretended to be returning from a run. I threw a confident wave to the guard at the gate and quickened my running pace. I didn't look back. No one followed.

Wearing Myra's wig in Florida's late-afternoon heat was torturous. I jogged the twisting, mile-long road. Several golf carts patrolling the lanes passed by. I rounded the bend with the big Cypress trees and body stumbled to a halt. Frozen in fear, I couldn't continue. The world rocked beneath me.

La Gringa

In front of me was my greatest fear, a living nightmare. Police cars were scattered in the driveway and spilled into the street. No one was outside; just an eerie silence with occasional ominous calls from the caged birds in backyard.

What's he being arrested for? It can't be smuggling. He was so cautious in how he operated. Youseff kept me insulated from his other, possibly shady, business practices. I had no idea what else he was involved in. He mentioned cattle farms in central Florida, construction businesses in the Panhandle, real estate holdings in the islands, but we never went into details. Our conversations centered around the Latin American assignments and Connect2Health

He won't survive in jail. He's too nice. Ugh! Now Lucia won't have a dad. She'll grow up and have to make up stories to her friends why her dad won't be at her dance recitals. This wasn't fair. So many family members, friends, neighbors, even animals relied on him. Will they come looking for me?

Youseff kept it clean. Besides a pay-as-you-go phone, there were no links between us. No paper trail. No records of our visits. No digital communication. Nothing.

I'd feared there would be a day like this where all this would come to an abrupt halt. As of that morning, I'd accumulated one million six hundred thirty-two thousand dollars. My earnings were resting in several safety deposit boxes, overseas bank accounts, but mostly, laundered in the business of Connect2Health.

A young woman skipped out of Youseff's front door. She wore a tank top with the name of a local university. Without a glance at the police cars, she scooted into the back seat of a sedan waiting across the street.

51

With the statewide launch of Connect2Health, I lacked any mental bandwidth to worry about an upcoming federal indictment. I searched my boss' name online and skimmed the local news. I attempted to get ahold of Jared, but I couldn't reach him. I later found out why he was inaccessible, because he was on a weeklong *ayahuasca* retreat in Peru.

I spent three agonizing days of being distant at dinners with Connor and absent in conversations at work. I kept the phone Youseff had given me was nearby at all times, in hope I'd hear from him.

While folding laundry at my house, I heard an archaic beeping from my sock drawer — where I kept the cell phone Youseff would call. I snatched the phone.

"Hello?" I questioned, trying to see if I could hear the phone being tapped.

"You ready for your next assignment?" he asked.

He's trying to trap me! I didn't think he would actually bring me down with him. He did such a good job keeping the distance between us. Maybe he's taking a plea deal if he gets me caught?

"I think you have the wrong number," I said.

"Soluna, why are you acting so strange?"

I remained silent to see if he'd continue. When we began working together, he mentioned a code phrase. If he phoned me and said 'I need a vacation,' I must destroy the phone he had given me and never return to his house until I heard from him again. I waited for him to say the phrase, but he didn't.

Instead, he broke the silence. "Come outside! We're out front."

I peeked through the shade. Youseff stood holding the phone to his ear while leaning against the taxi. I turned off the lights and slid on a pair of flip flops. I exited my home cautiously, looking around to see if the authorities were hidden and ready to jump out to arrest me. I didn't speak.

"Good to see you too!" he said sarcastically. "Why did you not respond to my texts?"

I approached him slowly and shot him a distrusting look. "Is this a sting?"

"If this was..." He pointed to Snoop, who just sparked a spliff. "Would this be happening?"

My boss seemed confident. *He wouldn't bring me down with him. He just wouldn't.*

"Then why the hell were the cops at your house?"

"What are you talking about?"

"I stopped by a few days ago," I answered. "There were squad cars everywhere."

"You came to the house?"

I nodded.

"Oh! You're talking about on Sunday? The police were doing a photoshoot with the animals," he explained. "They're trying to improve their image with all the brutality cases in the news. Something about a calendar or a social media campaign..."

My paranoid delusions crashed, and I started to laugh uncontrollably and playfully hit him on the arm. "You had me freaking out. I thought you were arrested. I'd been..."

"*Tranquila*," he interrupted. "Let's go for a ride." His stern face suggested that whatever needed to be discussed was serious.

I locked my front door, and we hopped in the taxi. Before Snoop started the car, he passed back the dwindling blunt. Youseff took a hit, and I finished it.

Twenty minutes later, we pulled into a parking lot of a public marina with charter fishing boats who just returned from a long day. "Where are we?"

"When I was single, I used to keep a boat here," he explained in typical Youseff fashion, offering a nostalgic nugget instead of a straightforward answer. "It's my favorite place to think."

We exited the taxi. I took a deep breath of the salty air. Both the boss and I were hypnotized by the watercolor sky which peacefully exploded with peach and purple clouds. We walked in silence towards the sea. I turned to watch Snoop reverse and drive away.

"Uh, Youseff," I questioned. "What's going on?"

He placed his hard on my shoulder and said, "You're done."

"What?"

"You won't be transporting any more."

"But..." I stuttered. "I know I'm busy, but if you need me for any quick runs, especially the easy ones to Santo Domingo, I can still do it."

"No," he shook his head. "Sol, you're done. You have way too much to lose."

"But what about the business? You'll need more merchandise before the holidays, won't you?"

"Yes we do, but I've been training your replacement."

"You're replacing me?" I took a step back. "With who?"

"She's a bit younger than you...blonde..."

"Let me guess. Does she go to Lynn University?"

"How'd you know?"

"I saw her leaving your house."

He smiled. My boss seemed to derive joy when I knew something he didn't know that I knew.

"So what's her deal?" I asked. I was interested to know who'd be filling my shoes.

"She's a graduate student finishing up a degree in Special Education. Her parents unexpectedly passed away last year, so she's now the legal guardian of her two younger siblings."

Any jealousy that I felt vanished. Yousseff had a recipe for accomplices — unsuspicious-looking *gringas* who could think quick on their feet and, most importantly, who had a deep motivation and purpose, other than to use the money for themselves. He could have had his pick of women who knew a thing or two about diamonds, but people who liked diamonds weren't the right people to smuggle them.

"So what does this mean?" My voice cracked. Youseff, the Levenfiches, and Seth had become such a large part of my life. They were the people who knew the most about me and were always there for me.

"Smash your burner and toss it. Once things blow over, I'll find Soluna's business card." He continued, referring to me in third person. "I'll follow up with her about an investment opportunity I heard about at the Art Basel party."

No more weeknight dinners in Boca Raton. No more playing with Lucia and the animals in the backyard. No more washing dishes and late night chats with Mercedes. His home had become my second home. The Boca Raton residence was an alternate universe, not just of luxury but of love. All the opulence and gold-trimmed decor aside, what I'd miss most was feeling like I was part of a large extended family.

My bottom lip began to quiver. "What kind of timeline are we talking?"

"Sol, I have no idea," he said, and put his hand on my shoulder. "When the time comes, know you're always welcome. In the meantime, please understand the distance. It's for your protection."

I began to fidget with my chain, raising it to my lips. *What kind of shit is he into? Is this the last time I'll see him?* I stared at the fiery, golden sun slowly dipping into darkness and watch a flock of gulls graze the horizon in their northern flight home.

He continued. "Connect2Health needs a leader. Not someone who's distracted by reckless trips to the islands."

I smirked. "Who are you calling reckless?"

He knew me better than I knew myself. He had the foresight to understand the day would come when Connect2Health would be more valuable than smuggling. While I hoped for it, I wasn't entirely certain it would become a reality.

Over two years of working together, we'd grown comfortable sharing long bouts of silence with each other. We didn't exchange words but stood side-by-side during the final moments of daylight. The beautiful vista embodied sadness, success, achievement, but mostly, finality.

Snoop returned, parking the taxi and leaving on its lights. The high beams lit up a picnic table on which he set with lobster tails, raw oysters, and a six pack of beer. The hum of cicadas ruled the island and harmonized our final meal together as a team.

52

My body catapulted through the hotel's revolving door and entered the refuge of the air-conditioned lobby. Summers in New York seemed to be stickier than Miami. This year was my second summer spending it in the city, and I was not used to it. The cement and buildings held the heat while the beach and palm trees fanned it.

"Ms. Hill, you received several packages today," the concierge man called out. "I placed them in your room."

"Thank you, Scott," I told the older man who I had befriended in random conversation while he'd flag down taxis for me.

The hotel became my weekday home. Last year, Connect2Health received significant investment and hired a full staff for our new headquarters in New York City. While my residence was technically in Miami, I spent most weekdays in the Manhattan office overseeing our nationwide service.

I ascended up the elevator and entered my room to encounter several packages, pieces of mail, and a floral arrangement on the dresser. It was a long day of work with people I barely knew and impersonal conversations I had to entertain. I wanted to hear the voice of someone who would ask *how I was* and not *how the business was*.

I grabbed my phone and called. Connor picked up and said, "Hey birthday girl!"

"You didn't have to do this" I marveled at the flower bouquet filled not with romantic roses, but bright, cheery flowers. Connor and I had not been together romantically for years, yet we remained friends - supporting one another in the challenging endeavors of our new, separate lives.

"Come on," he said. "Thirty is a big deal!"

"So what's new with you?"

"Same old. I'm on a case with this local dealer doing who is doing some creative laundering." He chuckled. "Bottom line, people are nuts!"

"Are you guys planning a bust like that Russian guy?" The man that Connor and his team were interrogating when my friends and I returned from the bachelorette party was a criminal traveling by using a stolen identity. He was a drug dealer selling on the Silk Road who invested his earnings in cryptocurrency. He rode the Bitcoin wave and cashed out just in time, making tens of millions of dollars and never paid a penny in taxes. Due to Connor's discovery of what was found on his laptop at the airport that afternoon, CBP and the IRS were able to recover ten million dollars in back taxes.

"Sol," he paused. "You know that I only pulled that guy in the back because I didn't want to see you and the girls."

"What?" I asked and my heart beat quickened. *What does he mean?*

"I knew you were up to something."

"Up to something?" I stalled.

He was silent. The howling of a New York City police car screamed below. My heart began to thud. *I thought this was all behind me.*

"I figured the best way to get me and my supervisors out of the line was to pull someone who looked suspicious." My eyes widened and I stopped breathing. He continued. "Turns out the guy was wanted in Mexico."

The lucrative bust secured Connor's promotion and his current high-ranked position in the DEA. He was leading on a narcotics-focused unit in Texas and recently proposed to another agent, a woman who liked guns and wanted babies as much as he did.

I didn't say more and neither did he. *What did he know?* I was at a loss of words. I didn't know if I should deny it, explain it, or ignore it. Instead of choosing which approach to take, he decided for me. "Sol, relax. I knew it wasn't drugs so I didn't ask."

Did he know the whole time? How did he find out? Could I be sentenced to jail for things I did years ago?

"I mean," I stuttered.

"Stop. You don't need to say anything. Remember I didn't and still don't want to know," he assured and changed the subject. "So what do you have planned for your big day?"

My body released its tension, and I blinked for the first time that minute. *He really doesn't want to know. Had he been protecting me that whole time?*

"We're heading to Santo Domingo for the weekend," I answered. I opened my closet and rolled out my suitcase. After I hung up our call, I'd be heading to LaGuardia.

The only gem that I'd be bringing back from that trip would be the diamond that Seth would soon place on my ring finger.

Epilogue

The butterfly doors opened, and the car turned on. "Good afternoon, Mrs. Ramirez. Where are we headed?"

"To pick up the kids," I responded and sat. The doors automatically locked.

"The ride should be twelve minutes," my car said. "As you can see, I've picked up the dry cleaning and groceries. They were out of kale so I replaced it with brussel sprouts. I hope that is okay?"

"Of course. Thank you," I responded. The car began to move.

"I reviewed your upcoming calendar. Catherine's sixty-fifth birthday is in two weeks. Would you like to send anything?" inquired the robotic voice.

"Yes. Please send her a bottle of 2021 Pinot Noir from King Estate and an orchid."

"Yes, of course." A screen popped up. "You have one pending video message."

"Play."

"*Hola, mi vida!* I just got to the house. The renovations look incredible."

Seth spun around, showing off the newly refurbished waterfront home. The sunset off the Adriatic Sea glimmered through the window.

"Good news! The negotiations went quicker than expected, so I caught the first flight this morning."

He flipped the camera to his face which reflected the sea in his eyes. Despite waking up to his eyes every morning, they still caught me off guard. They were like a mood ring, ever changing and reflecting the variation of blue off whichever body of water he was near.

"I can't wait for you guys to arrive. Please give the kids a hug from me. See you soon! Love you!"

The car spoke. "Would you like watch again?"

"Yes," I said smiling. The video replayed.

"Would you like me to play the news?" asked the robot.

"Yes, please."

"Yesterday evening, marked the kick off of the Americas World Cup. Miami will host Germany versus Japan next Wednesday. Miami residents are encouraged to avoid using the MacArthur Causeway because the opening party will be at the Youseff Levenfiche Conservator on Jungle Island."

We pulled up at the school yard. The car doors lifted. I stepped out to find two kamikazes running towards me. Nico and Katarina, the recent kindergarten graduates, slammed into my wide open arms. I kissed them both on their heads.

"Mom, why aren't you at work?" questioned Nico.

"My students had exams this week," I responded, squeezing both of their hands. "Today was my last day, just like you guys." Summertime excitement filled the parking lot. Stir-crazy kids were ready to be released from academic confinement, and their parents were ready to retreat to their out-of-town vacation homes.

Across the parking lot, an adorable strawberry-blonde toddler bounced on her father's shoulders. He waved. It was hard to remember the days when Jared wasn't a dad. With his goofy, loving personality, he was born for the job.

As moms passed by, I shared several superficial, yet courteous smiles. It seemed the mothers never forgave me for not being around much during the twins' preschool years. My absence was interpreted by them as being an absentee mother. They would never understand the intricacies of selling a company, or how that year of intense work afforded me the luxury of the flexibility that I now enjoy. With technology and AI assistants to handle the tasks required of most stay-at-home moms, they had time to either pursue a passion or gossip. Unfortunately, most picked the latter.

The redundant conversations with the moms were predictable and dull. *But who was I to judge?* Maybe since I didn't take the time to find out each of their past, there's a chance I was not privy to their own interesting story. Maybe illegal, maybe not. Maybe fascinating, maybe not. Maybe unusual, maybe not. Some of their stories were bound to be outside of the stereotypical mold.

After all, no one would have guessed that this university professor and mother of two who wore yoga pants and hid behind designer frames on the school yard, used the money she made from smuggling to fund the expansion of her recently sold company. There's always more than meets the eye.

Katarina opened her backpack and pulled out a box. She placed a plastic crown on her head full of thick blonde curls.

La Gringa

"Look, mommy! Uncle Jared gave me this," she proudly stated and extended her arm, handing me a Pretty Pretty Princess board game.

La Gringa

Muchas gracias for reading *La Gringa!*

If you enjoyed the story, you're encouraged to:

1. **Tag** @LaGringa_novel in a photo of you reading it

2. **Leave** a review on Amazon, Kindle or Audible

3. **Send** Sidonia a note at lagringa.co/hola

La Gringa

Discussion Questions

While *La Gringa* is a fast-paced adventure throughout the Caribbean, the novel intends to have the reader reflect about deeper themes — identity, karma, stereotypes, and more.

Note: The discussion questions contain spoilers.

1. Illegal doesn't mean immoral, and immoral doesn't mean illegal. The split between good and evil runs through all of us. Youseff saves helpless animals, yet runs shady businesses. What are some qualities in people that are often so redeemable that they overshadow their illegal behavior?

2. The zultanite ring is a metaphor for the different sides to Soluna. Just like the gem, she shows different hues depending on the environment she is in. Do you have different sides to you that only certain people see? Are these different aspects of you difficult or easy to transform into?

3. In order to stick it to her male partners and lock up Ross, Catherine and Caitlin lead with bold actions rather than words. Do you have examples of people in your

lives who have stood up for justice with their actions and not just their words?

4. The story begins with Soluna in an uncomfortable predicament — tell on Ross and risk losing the Miami Project or stay quiet and continue working on the project that means so much to her. Before Catherine proposed the plan, what would you have done? Would you have handled the situation differently? If so, how?

5. Has your skin color or being from a particular background hindered you? Explain. Has your skin color or being from a particular background granted you privilege? Explain.

6. Moving to Miami catapulted Soluna into a entirely different culture than her conservative Saint Louis upbringing. Have you moved or lived somewhere that was foreign to how you were raised? Did the experience enable you to value something about where you came from? Did you learn something about yourself being away from home?

7. At Youseff's dinner table, there were unassuming people from all walks of life — a rabbi, zookeepers, housekeepers, and many others. Do you know someone personally who committed a crime and you had no idea of their illegal activity until they were caught?

8. Do you think Connor was aware of the real reasons for Soluna's incessant international travel? If yes, why did he not intervene? What were other karmic occurrences in the story?